What You Wanted

C. L. Lomas

Where has this book been to?

CM, Bath, UK
L. Prem - Norwich, UK 5/08/24

Copyright © C. L. Lomas, 2024

C. L. Lomas has asserted her right under the Copyright Designs and Patents Act 1988 to be identified as the author of this work.

This is a work of fiction. All of the characters, organisations and events portrayed in this novel are either products of the author's imagination or used fictitiously.

All rights reserved. No part of this publication may be reproduced or transmitted in any form or by any means, electronic, mechanical, photocopying or otherwise without permission.

Dedicated to the dreamers and the doers

Chapter One
John

Words were whispered to me in the night. I could see their form as I closed my eyes, but the darkness turned them to water, running through the gaps in my open hands.

I walked through worlds only accessed through the corridors in my mind, anxious to share these maps with others. I would wake and the world would fall from my feet, cursed by every moment stolen from me.

The morning would return, fresh-faced and shining. The birds sang of positivity, possibility and hope as their sharp sound crept through the gaps in my blinds.

As usual, I shut them out, a cushion firmly on the side of each ear before spitting into my famia. I watched as a fresh coffee appeared in front of me, cup and all released from its orb shape. As I sip, I swallow my sadness, happy the sun had returned to my sight. I could feel my skin strain into a smile. Perhaps today would be different.

I think this each morning and by the afternoon I give up. Each day is empty, filled with space to extend the self, to stretch into becoming somebody else, endless opportunities to be the best version of yourself. I was told that writing would bring this higher self out of me, yet each day, as we all do, I consult a small glass screen, the passion plaque, which tells me what I desire.

It takes my pulse, measures my blood pressure, and scans my eyes for brain waves. Doing this determines the depths of my desire, deciding how to guide me to make the most of my time.

Each day it tells me to write, and each day I am surprised and frustrated by this outcome. I try, I sit and stare at walls, I gnaw on pen lids and my nails. I have gone through several laptops in the past few years after beating them to a pulp.

Each day becomes the same thread of failure, the same blank page. My famia makes me fresh coffee, strong and hot, infused with inspiration that cools off before the first sip.

This paradox of passion, pursued but unfulfilled, deters me from my stories, leaving them all unspoken and myself unsettled.

In true times of despair, I let my mind travel to what used to be there, so full of ideas it was difficult to move, tripping over what-ifs, and getting lost in maybes.

I begin to think of all the stories that have been said and all those which will never be uttered. I look to everyone else on their steps toward success, all pursuing their own desires and doing so gracefully. All the shadows I stand in whilst trying to see the sun.

I had once been a successful writer, with my books on shelves that were not just in my sleeping section. I used to have fans, people frantically waving pens at me and reciting my stories back to me. I once had a Faceless for support, guiding me with what worlds to weave, telling me the words I wrote were wonderful.

Now I chew on ink and stare into the distance. Perhaps I was looking for something that had never really been there, wondering how to get something that I had never had, back.

Now the age of the word is over, it is all visual, motion, and audible. If a person cannot watch it or sing it, then it is not important to them.

The publishing Faceless became defunct, only fuelled by the majority's wants. They just stopped accepting the written word, anything written is just produced into something visual and moving. But still, I want to write, in a world where words are not read anymore this is my curse.

The duality of understanding the demands of your inner desire and the despair of understanding that these demands cannot be met unless others desire them is a quick trip to a dark destination. What's worse is I know I can be good at it, yet the only books upon my shelf are my own. I have my back to them as I try to write, they have betrayed me as I have betrayed them, both abandoning each other instead of buttressing.

I stare at the glass square, a little plaque of passion, I flick it with my fingers, frustrated that it utters no more insight into what I want. The older models made you stick your head in them, a flash of light against your eyes and a swab on your tongue as it scanned your brain to find what you fought for.

As a writer, I know I should want to write, but there are so many words it is difficult to know what order to put them in. I dip my hand into an unseen life, lending my ear to its edges, wondering what I'll hear.

Sat in the shuffling silence shared between a man and his beaten-up laptop, I started to hear whispers of what could be. I think of the parties I once hosted, the people I have met, and the lives they have lived.

After thinking of myself, the suits I used to wear, the drinks I used to be sick from, I think of my friend Jada, a singer, arguably the best one. I think of the perpetual party she had thrown over the past 2 weeks. How I had embarrassed myself as I tried to keep up with a previous version of myself only to end up pouring myself over careless faces.

I had to consult my Faceless, usually left to despair in silence, as I needed its support on outfit choices. My suits no longer fit me, the stitching stretching on the shoulders and tight on the thighs. I opted for some tailored trousers and my least-stained shirt.

I could have consulted the passion plaque to see if I truly wanted to go but I knew that the alternative would be just a slower form of torture, so I left, watching the end of my front garden swirl and shift into the street opposite Jada's dwelling.

Jada had done it again, her whole life a firework night, her footsteps synonymous with the sound of stiletto shoes and popping champagne.

She was at the stage now where strangers would claim to know her more than anyone else did. She couldn't leave her house without causing a commotion. She was an ethereal earthquake whose presence was felt for miles.

Jada owned the top-floor penthouse. She owned a section of the sky, the Basi, which she saw her face shone upon most mornings. Some guy called MILK joked they would create a Basi just for Jada. But he was right, each month Jada's name was up there so 3 weeks out of 4 we would dance to her music. Nobody ever tired of her sound.

The first week of the party was flooded with alcohol and drugs. All provided to save us from using our passion points and famias. We were serenaded with Jada's songs, either floating over us on a tape or live through the speakers as she caressed a microphone.

 She sat in a perpetual spotlight which she shared with others, who were simply made beautiful through association. Offering her success to those she appreciated the most. Even 7 glasses of champagne deep she thought it necessary to thank her Faceless for serving the drinks.

She shared the stage with her friends MILK, a rapper, and Anya, a choral singer. It was entertaining, it was engaging, it should have inspired me, but each sip simmered and then turned sour in my throat.

On that final morning, of that second week my head gave in. The alcohol on tap and relentless temptation of drugs had been fun at first but the price of painless pills was not cheap, and my passion points couldn't cover any more.

I had to excuse the constant calls for sapphire shots and cocaine races, thanking a sparkly Jada as I evaporated over firework faces and snuck out behind striking silhouettes.

Before the landscape started to swirl into a sphere of change, I took the time to look around, reminiscing of the time I once owned a penthouse, one not too far down from Jada's. I remember the parties I would throw, the book readings I would host, it all seems like a different lifetime ago. I think a footballer lives there now.

My head feels like tar in summer just thinking back to that. Skin full of sludge and blood thick, I had fallen into the front garden of my sleeping section. Unable to make it to the door, I spent the next day tucked between two bushes.

The laptop shuts off, its dark stare reflecting my blank one, a haunting message that I was not doing enough. If I couldn't even entertain myself doing what I supposedly loved then how could I entertain anyone else? I think of the faces I have seen, the ones I will never meet and from somewhere in between, I pull out a character.

Each day their passion plaque tells them to find happiness, to smile. Finding happiness is like navigating a labyrinth that taunts you with glimpses of its core before throwing you down another warped corridor where all of the lights have been shut off.

I start to write this world into reality. Crafting a problematic protagonist. He is constantly questioning what his happiness means rather than experiencing it like the songbird or the rain as it races to the ground like a lover.

In his final moments, when the world falls still and his mind is tumbling over itself he smiles, finding solace before his eternal sleep.

At first, I hold it up like a trophy, close to claiming it as my magnum opus before realising it is only 15,000 words. I have sat here for 10 hours, my eyes are folding onto each other. It's awful. It lacks structure. It lacks substance. I close the screen, the sad tap a bowing head, a gallant fighter.

Defeated, I spit into my famia, and it prepares me the food I want. Apparently, I am in the mood for a ploughman's with ready-salted crisps. I pressed on the plaque again, knowing it was too soon to sleep but too late to achieve much else. The word 'Walk' flashes onto its face. I opened the front door and the end of my path became the woods.

Green canopies and silver streams, whispering waterholes and beckoning branches. Mosaic strips of light and shadow intertwine to create a golden tapestry as I stroll through its emerald stomach.

Solace and silence, a world far away from myself and my desires. The only disruptions are welcome ones caused by birds coming home and deer frolicking freely.

Of course, I could want this, I always want to walk in the air and sing with the birds, but I want to be known more than I want to fade. Here I can feel freedom and understand why it has to be fleeting.

The scent of the foliage, the taste of the sun, the feel of the breeze through my fingertips, I will never be as talented as the world around me, but I can be thankful that I am here to experience it.

The woods were perpetual, their evergreen gowns washing over me like beautiful women. The breeze ran through my hair like long fingernails, the wind waltzing with me.

To walk here was to live again, to breathe deeply and feel reborn. There was so much beauty here, how could I steal the painter's brush and melt it down into words when they had already created such a visual smorgasbord of serenity that I could barely take in, let alone talk about.

If I tripped on the twigs I fell into a comforting eternity, a softer plane I could only dip into before returning to my bitter, grey reality. If I could write these woods and amplify their whispers what poetry would permeate through their leaves?

The sun is deep into the setting, its vermillion dress cascading over the rolling hills, saying goodnight to the birds and I know I have to walk home. I turn, take a few steps and I am back at the edge of my path.

I open the door to my whirring laptop screaming for me, I know it is starving and I have no art for it. I place my hand on the passion plaque and it tells me to sleep.

I want to sleep but I rarely do. A few hours of dark and knowing it to be so does not constitute a restful sleep, I am too bothered by the absence within me. It is always light when I do decide to shut my eyes and finally, I have that first taste of peace but, it is always too late to be full of it.

Just as I am descending into drowsiness, the passion plaque chirps, and within a few seconds a new song starts playing. I instantly recognise Jada's voice, she has done it again, she will be placed on the Basi for the next few weeks.

I listen to her vocals, like lilies, delicate but so powerful, they linger, leaving a mark after kissing you gently. She was throwing a party at her penthouse, and I was being texted to go.

I looked at the clock knowing her party would go on for at least another week and decided that, perhaps on this occasion, sleeping would be more suitable.

I will go in a few days.

Chapter Two
Jada

Ribcage rising, gently to begin with, like a smile in the first light of spring and then faster as the minutes paced, lapping me in the race for news. Success was expected of me. I had always been satisfied with my songs, seeing the smiles on faces in crowds, the friendships made and strangers finding lovers, that was success for me but everyone else expected to see me on the Basi.

The first time I saw my face projected onto the sky, heard my songs automatically playing through other people's passion plaques and had strangers approach me about how my songs had impacted them, I was grateful, my songs were being listened to, and they were being enjoyed. I was young, eager for my ego to be stroked and to find a connection.

Now, I am constantly watched by my image, looming over the smaller shadow of myself. She is everything I am supposed to be, she is everything I can be and have been. I am never alone, I am watched by everything that is expected of me, rather than having myself seen.

My Faceless approaches with the auto-alert, my breathing is rapid, a washing machine in its penultimate cycle.

"Singer, Jada's fourth album 'Phoenix' is going on the Basi for the next two weeks."

Every time I release something it is the same cycle of humiliation, hope and harmony. I place my palm on the centre of my chest and imagine it is the hand of my Nani. She holds my chin and whispers that she is proud of me.

I wipe my eyes and smile, thanking my Faceless, which has no concept of gratitude. I request it to send invites to the names listed in its database so I can prepare for a party.

The colours of my penthouse depended on the mood of the album. This one was about igniting your own identity, flying through the flames to make a show out of the fire, everything was orange and red, as strong and striking as the Phoenix.

My third album, called Waves, is about becoming a lighthouse in other people's lives, guiding them to safer waters. My entire penthouse had been painted blue, with a pool in place of the main floor.

Novelty balloons in the shape of phoenixes blown up and spicy margaritas made from my Faceless. My Faceless finished scrunching olive oil hair gel into my curls and zipped up my dress as I perfected my eyeliner. My usually desolate penthouse and I both dressed up for hundreds of eyes.

My backup singers and trumpeter arrive first with hands full of my favourite manuka honey and a bouquet of red roses. It remained quiet after that, as a few no-namers joined in, among a few familiar faces.

The music was at a good volume, people could comfortably converse but dance if they wanted to, and all of the food was flame themed as well as the shots.

On my third, my friends MILK, Anya and Ali arrived with more bottles of booze that they had already had half of.

"You are unbelievable! Jada's Basi isn't back because it never left!" said MILK

"I am seriously so proud of you!" said Anya

Ali shuffled on the spot, handing me a rose "Sappho would be proud of all you have achieved"

I hugged them, happy to see a set of friends in the smog of smiling strangers.

"Shots?"

Two days into the party and there were still a few faces missing. Perhaps seeing a projection of mine in the sky was enough for them, maybe seeing this smiling shape, a sentimental silhouette in the clouds made me real to them, to see me was to know me, even if I couldn't see you.

Slumped on the sofa with a shot in my hand and a firm smile on my face, I couldn't help but think it was all too much as a firework flew through the spacious apartment before exploding into the shape of a phoenix in flight.

Of course, this was met with an eruption of applause and calls for more, but I drowned it out, staring at the piles of sick spilt over the shoes strewn around the floor.

Cigarette butts on the balcony and scattered broken bottles a statement of a loose celebration. My once pristine counters are now chalky with remnants of cocaine and littered with straws.

Frantically, my Faceless was trying to keep up but people had started to trip it up, throwing drinks over it. I caught one of the nameless people shamelessly making out with its head, touching its metal body as though it were a magnet. Horrified and haunted, I had to put it back into the cupboard as the mess ensued.

I didn't know how to clean it up myself and neither did anybody else here. I flicked the cigarette butts off the side of the balcony and filled a sink with soapy water for the shoes whilst my party guests continued to delve deeper into derailment.

A fight had broken out between a couple of nameless faces. They were being applauded by a crowd that was gaining numbers. Fists were being thrown and cheers were being called.

I didn't condone this sort of behaviour in my home so wrestled my way through the watchers and broke it apart, scalding the fighters for doing so at my party.

The atmosphere had stagnated, and guests were vanishing at the door. This night was supposed to be about me, about my connections, it was meant to be a celebration.

I approached the microphone, taking a deep breath in before starting to sing to distract everyone from their drinks, my backing singers harmonised with me from their spots around the room before finding me on the window stage.

Then I saw John standing with a drink in the crowd and the smell of the sick seemed to evaporate. I smiled as I sang a little bit louder.

Chapter Three
John

She hit her final note and wiped a tear from her cheek, everyone was cheering, their eyes committed to her frame as she stepped onto the piano and exclaimed she had a speech.

"As you know my album Phoenix has just been released". This was met by more applause and a few appreciative whoops.

"It has already gone to the top! I have so many muses, whether it be the mirrors, the wounds of words thrown at me, or the worries in the eyes of others. Together we weaved this album, it is ours. I know you want to dance, drink, do a few drugs if you are that way inclined, so let's listen and have a good time!"

She was hoisted down from her piano by a group of smiling women as her song began to filter out of the corners of the room, creating an ethereal mist that caused everyone to start moving.

After an hour of invisibility and awkward head nods at passers-by Jada approached me, her long arms wrapped strongly around my shoulders.

"I am so relieved you're here!"

5 glasses of spicy margaritas down I could only nod.

"How do you like the song?" She said gesturing to the speakers.

"It's good, powerful, poignant, it has an uplifting beat, you can see why it is on the Basi."

'That is very kind of you. Anything I can get for you?"

I did a quick glance around the main room, the stench of alcohol permeated, the state of the sick and the obnoxious colours. I declined knowing if I had another drink I would only be adding to the mess.

"How are you?" she said, as she popped a painless pill to allow her to keep drinking without being sick.

I chuckled, staring at the toes of my worn brown shoes, and noticing the hem of my trousers had snagged on something.

The margaritas had gone to my head and pushed the words that didn't fit in my mouth out into the air between us.

"You know Jada I am very happy to be here, you are so effortless in what you do. I am hoping that at some point soon I can host you at a Penthouse again. I have started writing again."

She smiled at this, a stronger sparkle behind her eyes.

"That is brilliant to hear John, what about?"

I pitched the more concentrated version of what I had been producing to her, embellishing certain details, lamenting that I could not translate my words into a written format as they evaporated into the drunken fog.

I was tripping up over my words, panicking to get a lie out as a truth. If I sounded good enough, perhaps I would become it.

"I am excited to see the film when it is finished, and for the release party at your penthouse," She was genuine, her smile full of hope as she sauntered off.

Penthouses were only for people who had made it onto the Basi. I had indeed thrown a party, with Jada and a few friends. We had all made ourselves quite sick and silly from too many sapphire margaritas.

The Faceless had yet to make the painless pill so I struggled to remember the fun. I vaguely recall the sickness afterwards, especially standing here and seeing it simmer in the sunlight.

I stood alone in a crowded room full of success stories none of which could be shared with me. When you are standing with giants you realise how small you are. I wandered around, disgustedly impressed by the size of her place. 10 rooms for one person and 3 were party spaces.

I walked past her vast music room and home studio, her bedroom, a room just occupied with one central stage and a dancefloor and then a contrastingly small room that I stumbled into.

 Just big enough for two large bean bags, a rug, and an odd box. The odd box contained essential oils, a photo album with some older lady, and a little Jada, at the bottom was a dog-eared book. My own, Synthetic Skies. I flicked through a few of the pages to find she had lovingly annotated certain sections, highlighting her favourite quotes.

'As she watched the sky fall, she finally felt the floor beneath her. She had always known this would be the way and that she would be the one to do it, she had to do it alone.'

 After I had allowed another few glasses of champagne to be poured directly into my mouth, I had a few more sips of margarita and awkwardly joined a group of people too far gone to realise I was not one of them. as we sang through Jada's discography I stumbled for the exit. Closing Jada's apartment block door, feeling the city morph to spit me back out at the sleeping section.

I was too drunk to know where exactly I wanted to be. I just knew I wanted to be asleep. As I hit the grass and threw up on some bushes I realised this was not my house catching a blonde lady watching me from the window in concern. Her sleeping section and the bushes in the front were the same as mine, the same in shape and structure.

 Cloned homes and cloned lives, we are all the same, all wanting to be different. I tried to pull my head out of my thoughts but faded into myself to avoid the sight of my sick.

Then it happened again, all over the rose bushes that every other house had. As I wiped my chin I realised the woman was peeking her head out of the window.

"The door is open."

As soon as I found myself navigating the wobbly room and collapsing on the beige sofa, I finally fell asleep, head full of success stories that were not mine, that I could not write.

Sick simmered in my throat as I woke to the smell of fresh coffee. Peeling open my eyes I was convinced I was back in my sleeping section before I noticed that the bookcase had been replaced with a bird poster. I swallowed the sick, remembering the shame of vomit that had stained this stranger's garden.

"Oh gosh, good you are moving, I was worried, you have been asleep for 16 hours." said the stranger

"Sorry", I had to pick my head up off my shoulders in order to sit up.

"I don't usually get like this, I just didn't take the painless pills. Do you have any? Don't think it will be successful at this point, but I am desperate."

"What's that?"

I shook my head, feeling it fall back into the corners of my skull.

"Um, I'm Jill by the way"

"John", I replied.

"So how come you ended up on my lawn and not your own?"

"I don't know, usually, I get back to my sleeping sections, I am really sorry I must have just gotten confused."

"It is no bother, just have to be gone before Mark, my husband gets back", her voice fading as she saunters off to the kitchen.

"Do you mind if I use your famia?"

She came through with it, an older model which meant it would only be programmed at 60% accuracy and 40% quality.

I thanked her nonetheless.

"Please be careful with it, it was a present from Mark." I watched as she walked back into the kitchen.

I delicately spat onto the square slide and watched as it brought back a dry hamburger with stale bread, cold chips, and water. It churned in my stomach, tossing and turning, like waves out at sea.

Forcing myself to my feet, I walked into the kitchen to bid Jill goodbye and return her famia to find her sipping coffee and watching the birds.

She was half swallowed by the lumpy armchair, but her gaze was focused on the trees outside.

My house did not have trees in the back garden, my back garden was a thin sheet of patio with a chair for when I had my smoke. I approached her and then realised she was talking to herself, counting the birds as they darted between dwellings.

"10 chaffinches, 4 goldfinches and, gosh too many blue tits to recall, at least 3 more than yesterday." She exclaimed, scribbling this down in her notebook.

"Ooh another robin, a blackbird, and that green one, that little one, what is it called?"

She scrunched up her face in confusion.

"It's a greenfinch. I read a book on birds a few years back when I was trying to write a story about the artist who made paintings by throwing birds dipped in ink onto canvases", I advised.

She blinked at me, a look of shame and disgust fell behind her eyes for a moment, as she crossed out a little green one and wrote greenfinch.

"I can get you the book if you want?"

"No, no that's fine, I am not a big reader"

"Why are you counting the birds?'"

Her face turned grey, her green eyes looked to the floor for a second before returning her gaze to the sky.

"Because they are beautiful, and I am glad I am able to share my home with them. I want to make sure that as many as possible are visiting. Mark grew me this garden, he built me that bench", she said pointing at an elaborate oak seat in the centre of the garden. "I am going to enjoy it".

"Impressive"

"That's where he'll be now, always busy, so busy."

My stomach had started to settle so I sat down on the round wooden dining chair close to the window. This sleeping section looked like mine but felt emptier, colder almost.

Despite its accents of vibrant colour, the building felt as though it was breaking, its beating heart slowing down. I could feel it didn't want me there, its blank walls watching me fearfully.

"What do you mean exactly?"

"He'll be at the projects, probably making a bridge or a bench. He is a builder"

"A builder? But the Faceless do all that, constructing whole museums in a weekend, why doesn't he focus on what he wants to do?"

"That is what he is doing, the Faceless created the projects for people like him, you know the act of creation is quite a popular passion. He builds all sorts. He even provided the Faceless with the blueprints for the Liatrium"

I stared at her, suppressing my laughter, this could surely not be a thing, physical labour? Who would want that?

"Honestly, he'll come home smelling of cement or wood, be drenched in sweat but have a massive smile on his face as he tells me what he has been building. He always says one day they'll let him help build a museum, think he just has to build a few more bridges"

"Hmm, that could be exciting, anyway, thank you for this.' I handed her the famia. Thank you for looking after me and I am so sorry again for your front lawn."

"Oh don't worry about that, I never go out there anyway."

"Well I'll see you later and oh think I have just seen another chaffinch."

"No I have got that one already thank you."

 Before I left I took in my surroundings. Each sleeping section was the same, all designed with the rectangular lounge, beige sofa, and wide flat screen. Each square kitchen with its 5 cupboards and table, all yellow brick and bleak with the same T-shaped path and rose bush that never blossomed on the front.

 Each house bore some shadow of the predominant presence that subsided in its structure. Jill's had an ornament of a robin on each windowsill and a carpet of suet crumbs in each room, and I had my busy bookshelf and blinking laptop, but all the skeletons were the same.

The world swirled and I was back in front of my sleeping section. It looked as scrawny as I felt. I wish I could strip my skin off, wring it out, and start again.

Surrounded by my paper trophies, my sore head took me back to my days on tour. Camera flashes replaced faces, capturing my own stunned smile, screaming young adults fawning over me, the pen I had chewed at for months now a companion signing my name on my own books.

The stories I had choked on until the early hours, now flapped at me like flags in the wind, each one a territory of triumph.

 I fingered the creased spine of Synthetic Skies, remembering my character who was always watching, floating my fingers flicking through my famed triumph, the Stellar Chronicles.

I remember the relentless questions, probing about the production of my words. How is it done, how do you think, what's next? What's next? Never, what's now? Never, what's this?

The ghosts of this time are still very much alive in the halls of my mind, with their knives and daggers carving out my life. I don't know how it was done. I just did it, sitting at my desk, tapping my pen, or staring at a screen. I screamed until the story unfolded.

I used to know what to say, what to write, how to smile in a way that meant I was worthy of being wanted and now there is nothing. The Island that success will send you to is a harrowing one full of ghosts of people who swore they were your friends.

Sore head in hands I knew it was time. Sitting with my glass companion I began to write. I thought of Jill, her devotion to her husband, her focus on the birds, out of all the faces I had met, the titles, and the names I had come to see in the sky, it was hers watching up for the clouds, that spoke to me the most.

I knew all the words in the world, I knew this was what I wanted, and this felt right. Each question deserved an answer, and it was time to start talking.

Each divulged into my desires, each magnifier into my psyche, it was time to do something differently. I weaved worlds between my fingertips, sat on the same beige sofa I travelled to interspace, into strangers' heads, a fly in my character's lives.

An afternoon later, I had tapped into existence the beginning of a soon to be bestseller, a love story not thought of before, both end up getting what they want but neither of them is happy. The girl falls in love with the other, but the boy wants him to herself.

It was good, but I could never be sure if it would be good enough. My first book had made it on the Basi. It was only for a week but that ushered in a storm of applause, ovations, and congratulations from strangers in the streets, that saw my name broadcasted on TV.

That was almost 20 years ago. I feared this would be nothing for the Faceless now but that was no reason not to try.

I wanted to be a writer again, I wanted to not only walk the halls of the museum in the city but to be on its very walls.

Chapter Four Jill

With John gone I settled back into the silence, the house humming with harmony that it was once again left undisrupted, waiting patiently for all of its rightful dwellers to return.

The day moved slowly now, as the birds flew through it, unaware of their beauty and their defiance to exist just how they wished to. From meeting Mark, I had decided to do just as they did and live solely to enjoy their existence.

I had never used a passion plaque, only knew of their existence through Mark, I had never wanted anything other than for his love and peace. I learned quickly that just because you want something does not mean you will get it.

 I am happy when there are birds by my window, a good TV show to kill the hours, and when Mark is back by my side. That is enough.

I sat in silence and called it peace even though a held breath could never be the same as a smile. After a while of counting the same birds, I picked myself up and walked through to the lounge, the beige couch still frowning with the weight of John's ghost.

I smoothed it out, raiding the cupboard for some sort of scent that would remove the evidence of his existence. Mark wouldn't understand that the only arms I wanted around me were his. I would wear him like a scarf even if we lived in a perpetual summer.

After swatting John out, I sank into his shape and made it my own, flicking through the TV shows to fade into before the day died.

Light hearted, love and drama, I could lose myself in the scandals of others as I sipped in silence, laughing at those who were so loud. They were all similar iterations of each other; over the top, oozing with sex and beautiful bodies that could not be real when looking at mine.

Some wanted to be these people, their passion plaque telling them they wanted to be watched, they wanted to be thinner, they wanted more passion points, doing anything they could to be who they wanted.

I never understood how you would want to change yourself, you'd have to actively do something to create it, and you couldn't just get it because you wanted to.

The carved contestants always had to partake in incredibly ridiculous challenges to impress their attractive partner; from public humiliation to performance validation, I was entranced by their sexual squalor and rampant rebellion.

On my third show of the day, as the losers were being announced, Mark arrived. I was always bewitched by his glistening arms, the sweat a sure sign of a successful project, crumbs of brick in his palms and golden skin. He was the centrepiece in every room.

I flung myself into his arms, his chiselled body engulfing mine, as he waltzed me back to the sofa before kissing me passionately and then peeling me off.

"I know, I know it's been a while, but my god has it been worth it? Bloody bricks, I love it Jilly, never ever have I been happier than when I'm down there, with my mates, a tinny and a vision. And boy did we deliver. It was a bridge. We've had them before, not too difficult, there were some quite intricate features but overall, it is just a little olive branch in stone. Guess how long it took us? Go on, ha you'd never do it, 4 days!"

He had been gone for 7. I wondered for a second where he'd been for the rest of the time if it had only taken one day but decided to smile it away instead. To see him shine like this, excused him for his time away.

"I reckon this one will stay up, remember when the bench stayed up? It is still there now Jill, if only you would come and see it, that doesn't matter, I could build you one here, for the garden for your birds?"

He had done this several times now, destroying the previous one as he always had a new idea, a new concept as to how a basic bench should actually look.

I smiled at him with a thin, curved line of acquiescence.

"Well, I love the other one I have, but of course my dear, I would love that one all the same."

"I'm not counting the foundation we did that last week, but the actual building, that was today! One day Jill, we are unstoppable."

He spoke about the girder placement, the railings they had used, the intricacy of the decking plan, and dismantling the bridge to rebuild it in his mind.

 I was his willing and doting audience, chewing on his words despite my show now shut off and some spin-off series spiralling into its final episodes as he wrapped up his story.

Then it was bedtime. I was a little tired but enthralled as always by Mark's encompassing embrace, his skin swallowed me whole as I allowed him in.

His skin was salty from his day, mine was pale and limp, he kissed it all and made me beautiful with his touch. With each caress he took back the time he had been gone, kissing each absence into bliss.

We both buzzed with each other's bodies, skin bouncing on skin until the final petals folded, and the first bird sang. We collapsed into each other, stopped only by the finale of our actions.

He had beaten me to the first look of sunlight. I joined him downstairs. He was looking at the sky before smiling at my presence.

"Loads of them out there today Jill, even the sun has joined them. Why don't you sit outside with them? Have a little sing like you used to."

I nodded quietly at him. On better days I would do just this, dipping my toes on the grass and sitting outside in the sunshine as the birds sang. Other days, after I had counted them, I had to shut it out.

He wrapped his arm around my waist and kissed the top of my forehead before pushing his thumbs into his passion plaque.

"Haha again, build, don't even know why I still use this thing."

I smiled meekly at him. Just because he wanted to do something didn't mean he should go and do it.

"It is a really sunny day, do you want to sit out with me for a while?"

"Come on Jill, clearly, I want to build."

"What is there for you to build? The Faceless do it all". The words collided, collapsing on top of each other as they fell from my mouth.

"So, you are saying what I do doesn't matter because it doesn't last? Jill, I am doing what I want. I know what I want, what do you know?"

"You are right, I am sorry. you are pursuing your passions and for that I am proud of you, I just miss you desperately. You aren't here and when you are it is only for a moment."

"Because I am doing stuff Jill, I am providing for you, I am proving myself.'

"And I am sorry that that pressure must upset you, but I promise you, you have done enough for me."

"You don't upset me, Jill, you just disappoint me, you drag me downwards, you refuse to try a passion plaque, accepting that to sit and wait is all you want to do."

"All I want to do is to be with you Mark, I don't need a machine to tell me that, I have my heart."

He smiled at me then, the redness leaving his cheeks, his fists returning to hands.

"I know you do Jill and I love you, but this is what I want to be doing so please let me do that, I will see you soon."

I had to count the birds. He was right, there were more this morning, with my chipped mug I sat outside and counted them all. I flicked through my notebook of birds.

45 Chaffinch, 10 blue tits, a robin, and a bird I hadn't seen before. It had a beautiful golden face with a sharp beak and wings that seemed to emanate the forces of the waves, the way the feathers were stacked upon each other, fragile on their own but a force when fused together.

I had only seen this sort of pattern a few times before, staring at the sea at the edge of the horizon or sometimes as I settled into a TV show, the waves would find me.

The bird's song startled me out of my space. It's a tune so melodic and repetitive, yet full of range, a constant voice from the smallest soul singing about absolutely nothing but doing so as if it was the most important thing to it.

Mark still wasn't home, who knew when he would be and there were no good shows on until later. I hovered by the front window, cowering behind the curtains. Nobody. I stripped naked and lay in the back garden, birdseed in both hands, I was still.

I chewed the seeds out of my fingernails afterwards, admiring the beak pecs and claw scratches that echoed on my palms. The pain only nature could provide, the pain I had intentionally caused myself, born out of love and service to care, I smiled.

Wet hair stuck to my shoulders. I scrubbed at my skin with a coarse towel. Gracing my body with a white top and shorts I draped myself on the sofa, mid-afternoon had arrived, and my shows were ready to watch.

Chapter Five
Will

Into my later adolescence and my years spent as a young adult, my days were full of unbuttoned shirts, loose ties, and multiple women, poured over me like the lavish champagne on our lips.

My hours were a drug-infused haze, as I happily absorbed my parents' riches, their greatness excusing my indifference to becoming a whole person. I didn't know or care what I wanted, I just knew to be wearing sunlight and the sweat of many lovers was enough to get me through the day.

Celebrities had penthouses but I had an estate. My whole life could exist within this space and all I had to do was ask for it. We had Faceless for everything. When they were not cleaning up our sick, making our food, or creating cocktails they would make my clothes for me. Clothes that I would then burn just for fun, or that I would throw at my friends just for something to do.

My friends would fight them, cheered on by the rest of us, all drunk on spirits and laughter. Sometimes you would see individuals sneak off with them, using them for more intimate purposes, sometimes you would see groups, sometimes they wouldn't sneak off at all and the full coitus would rile around in front of you as limbs wrestled with wet metal.

All that did this would claim they did so because they could have whoever they wanted simply because they wanted them. The Faceless were thoughtless, feelingless vaults existing, initially, only to respond to our wants, enabling this descent into debauchery. I was never as depraved to do that as I didn't want to sleep with something that couldn't respond to my power.

There were breaks in this routine, we had no painless pills yet and my friends had homes to go to so between the drugs and the women I would fill my days with literature from one of my parent's many libraries. I filled my head with fantasies wondering how far I could stretch my reality to reflect the words that I had digested.

I once made my Faceless strip out one of my parent's halls to replace it with an indoor forest so my friends and I could play hide and seek in the woods without getting rained on.

People loved me for it. I was a firecracker. I provided some sun behind their clouds. If nothing was going on I would make it happen. Every occurrence was an excuse for a party. A marriage, a half-moon, or even a random Wednesday in June.

If someone broke a glass or an old vase, we would all cheer and join in. We would rip pages out of books and shower each other with them, we would set fire to old rooms just for the thrill. We were always up from sunrise to sunset but were always too busy, dancing or drinking to notice its beauty.

I didn't leave my estate until late into my twenties. Slowly, fewer sleeping bodies were left stretched out on the sofas or entangled together in one of the many bedrooms as my friends started to change their minds about what they wanted.

No longer were days full of gold and glory but something to fill the gaps between the glasses and laughter, being taught by the Faceless what they wanted to hear; that they were worth more than this and deserved to have what they wanted. This entitlement was reinforced to them through a Faceless creation called a passion plaque.

Echoes of my youth understood this need to pursue something but now all I needed was to have fun. At first I laughed at them, telling them that this is all they could ever want, to drink, to dance, to kiss, isn't that all that matters? Why would you want anything more than all you can have?

My friends couldn't explain the feeling to me but the opportunities the Faceless had shown changed their experience at my events.

After scouring the remaining books for more enticing ideas to bring people back to the party, I put fireworks in the wheels of the Faceless, delighted as my friends whooped as its shiny body flung through the chandelier and up onto the roof in a beautiful green and gold explosion.

I was disappointed with their ambivalence towards the Faceless duel and the Faceless live band. They were bored and I was out of fun books, left with dusty copies of a different life that I had not got around to living in yet.

Eventually, I was left alone, drinking with Faceless who could not help me as I didn't know what I wanted. Now the party had stopped, I was the only one that longed for it to go on. I drank alone, sobbed alone, watching myself make the mess and watching how the Faceless rushed to clean it up.

 Their incessant need to please and cater suddenly made them pathetic, pitiful, and problematic. They plagued me with dependence, I was unable to do anything other than ask them.

Drinking Château Lafite Rothschild straight from the bottle, I was bored and wanted to see other people. I decided to leave the estate, stumbling down the amber gravel driveway and tripping over the marble cobblestones.

I walked through the acres of greenery before feeling the space shift before me, twisting into a place full of tall buildings and people. The experience was unsettling, leaving me clutching the wet tarmac and struggling up to my feet. A large sign read 'Welcome to the city of Endsville'.

The streets were busy, full of people who were wearing sharp suits, or stained shirts, stilettos, and stylish trainers. I realised I was wearing father's old trouser bottoms and a thick dressing gown, my hair unwashed and eyes heavy, hands still clutching the bottle.

 No one noticed me as they weaved their way in and out of their own worlds. Fuelled by drunk generosity, I offered a few sips of my wine, but each refused so I kept on walking.

A smorgasbord catering to wants, traditional restaurants, Liatriums where you could watch the latest films amongst other leisure's, a hairdressers, and one small shop selling bizarre food items. All were run by Faceless.

The buildings were tall and inspiring, something was happening here, something that called back to a former life I once looked at longingly.

I walked further on finding myself down alleyways littered with boozers with all the drink but none of the joy. I finished the last sip of wine and tossed it aside hearing it shatter down an alley. Startled by the noise of my own doing I turned around to see its shape.

Then I noticed the children. Frail looking and filthy I approached them with concern. Skeletal faces with threatening eyes, arms that have never been held, foreheads never kissed and stomachs never full

They snap their teeth at my smile, cower as I approach, or come at me with knives and brandish the shards from my broken bottle at me.

I persist, trying to give them Faceless crackers from my pockets, instead, they try to take everything, threatening me further before relenting as they realise I have nothing left to offer. I do not feel anger, I feel shame that this has been allowed.

I returned to them a few times, coming back to the city to leave them food bundles when they were out of sight before watching them from afar when they returned. No one else seemed to notice, no one else offered a hand.

Children are made like a point, their purpose is to make something of their maker and when this isn't done, they are no longer wanted. Parents think that to deliver them is enough, to love them more than yourself would be too much.

With nowhere else to go, the streets swallow them whole, leaving what is left of their humanity to morph into whatever it takes to survive. Killers are pitiful creatures, born out of greed and forced to live with scraps.

I would try to speak to them, approaching them slowly, crouching down to their height, and whispering "hello". The youngest ones hissed at me whilst the older ones brandished weapons or jeered at me, forcing me to keep my distance.

When we fail our children we fail our own futures but the Faceless protect us, fixing our feelings and blinkering us from our own negligence.

They were alone, they defied all those who wished them dead, they were feared but we had created them. They filled the streets with shame and rage, a constant conflict.

Many people didn't want to see the truth so rarely saw this sickening sight, but I saw it and I wanted the Faceless to see what they had done, knowing the monsters you make are only reflections of yourself.

Chapter Six
John

Everything I am belongs to the air. All of the words float above me, spoken by others claimed by thieves. Repurposed and processed into something more digestible, a film, a TV series, an advert, a song to sing and not understand.

My feet stand on ground that is prepared for a ruinous earthquake, always waiting for the cracks to swallow me whole. Met with another rejection, perhaps it is my footsteps that unsettle the Earth. I attempt to shift its foundations, but the world isn't ready to move yet.

Why write words for no one to see? Why write a world for people who will not read? When eyes do not see, how can I be?

I place down my pen, knowing its touch for the last time, I close my laptop hearing its lids touch, a kiss of goodbye.

The power of the masses outweighs the power of my passion. My words are drained to palpable liquid, a quick hit that leaves no lasting impact. My story is merely a sentence about something they want to sell. I have offered up my soul, always questioning what it is worth.

I refuse to ask the passion plaque what now, what's next, what do I want for myself? I feel it in my boiling blood that I must drink. I push away the door and pull myself into the breeze, following its grace I am in the city. I see the Liatrium full of film, full of clips, no paper cuts in their sore eyes.

I am aware as I walk through these triumphant walls that I am being watched with an uneasy eye of small bodies in the shadows. Their skeletal silhouettes stain the corners of the city. I see them staring and am thankful for the light.

Although frail, I know these feral things will devour me if I stop. I don't have my Famia on me so I can't even throw them food.

Without pausing I take off my jacket and throw it to them, quickly stumbling into the closest bar to have a liquid kiss.

I order a dark one from the Faceless behind the bar which serves it quickly, cold, and refreshing. Liquid, liquid, liquid, oh how to win is liquid.

I sat at the back and had another, checking my passion plaque for auto-alerts to determine how wide my smile should be.

There was nothing at home for me, no more stories, no lover, no dependents. Right now, the only thing that has justified my existence is the bartender and the bitterness of my beer in my throat.

I sat with my third for a while, perturbed by how many people had been in here when I came and were still here now, sat with similar strangers sharing the same stories drinking themselves into deafness.

Men with red faces and women with grey eyes. Some bodies were on the floor, bleeding, asleep, possibly dead, no one seemed to care. Voices were raised and drinks were lowered. Fists met faces and lips met glass.

 I am standing on a cliff, quite far from the edge but close enough to see it and each day I am unwillingly pushed towards its abyss and there is nothing I can do to stop it. I cannot write my way out of this inevitable drop, I cannot hold the hand of the pusher and plead with them to stop, for a day, or for an hour, to please just stop so I can take it all in, so I can breathe again and admire the view before the fall.

I am always alone on this cliff, averting my eyes from the edge but I know it is there, I can feel its glare. No comfort, or anger just cold knowing that whatever I do I will one day have to join it.

I order another pint then order everyone else one.

"People in here don't usually do that" some woman said from behind her pint.

"Why?"

She shrugged "I guess people in here don't have the power to do that, you'll probably end up on the floor if you do that."

I sat with myself for a while and tried to scrape sentences off the ceiling of my mouth, I tried to make sense of what it had all been about. I think of Jada, of her new single, of how through her voice she will go on, there is no cliff edge for her, just clouds.

I let the foam dissolve on my chin as I chuckle thinking about her last performance. I didn't go, I should have.

I had seen footage of her latest show, I mean who hadn't by now? She had fireworks on her dress that exploded whenever she hit a high note, she had doves leave the chest pockets and fly over the crowd. She was younger, she was hungrier and eventually, I admitted to myself that, she was just all in all better than me.

She knew me when I was no one, she was born someone but still, she had been the one to infuse my life with hers, following me into the Liatrium on the day we met, many years ago. If I was her I would have just kept walking.

I looked at my fingers, still black and smudged from a previous self. I felt the haze of wasted yesterdays and the rough rock of unfamiliar futures pass over me and decided it was time to go home.

I must have floated home as I don't remember my feet touching the floor. I fell into the forest instead of the sleeping section, perhaps this was my calling, to live as free as a leaf in the autumn breeze but even the leaf cannot see how tethered it is to the mighty tree, how it is destined to fall to the floor and disintegrate into nothing over time.

The ruinous roar of my final pint bellowed from within me, I hit the ground, a fallen city, face down between loose branches and hedgerows. I did not move until the sun woke me the next morning.

Chapter Seven
Florence

I was born on the red carpet, my beginning applauded by a thousand flashing lights. Flo Rose, a fully-fledged actress after just 2 roles all achieved by the age of 19. I was living the life that myself and everyone else wanted, and now being seen was my success. I was known by strangers, unstepped streets would become my spot lit stage if my heeled feet kissed their cobblestones.

I had a bounty of passion points but that didn't matter, they were just accessories to my identity, my shoes, my clothes, my food, everything I was given was always free because my image sold better than passion points could buy. I was a mirror to others saying, 'You are all you will ever be, and I am all you will ever want to be'.

Each tooth scrubbed and shaped to perfection, each hair arduously curled into place yet exuding effortless grace. Each word poised and perfected, myself scripted. Just as I had wanted it all to be.

All the other celebrities here tonight are wearing gowns and get-ups sewed by the Faceless, I had actual people begging to make a dress for me. In the end, I had asked my Faceless to tell my fans to send in pieces of their favourite clothes so that my Faceless could weave them into a dress for me to wear tonight.

One garment made out of 300 others, each piece once a fan's beloved item of clothing, now moved with me. As I graced the carpet, face a glow, posing for the pictures, a Faceless bot rolled over to me.

"Florence-Rose, what is it like to be here tonight?"

"Well, this is my 9th red carpet of the season, so boring if anything", I laughed, "Do these things get longer? I have quit the gym, red carpets are now my cardio."

Faceless didn't laugh so I was unsure how this would have been received through broadcast.

"No, no I am ever grateful to the fans that got me here, the films I have been a part of it is always incredible to see something you want coming to fruition."

"What do you want this film to say to your fans?"

"Be adventurous, seek opportunities and say yes."

"Do you ever feel you are somewhere you are not supposed to be?"

This question startled me, and an uncomfortable claw crept up the nape of my neck. Shaking it off I continued to smile as I stared back into the unseeing orb of the bipedal shape.

"Sorry, could you repeat the question?"

"What would you say to those who don't know where they want to be yet?"

'Oh, of course! I think it is natural to sometimes feel you do not belong in a place you are supposed to be in, but as you develop and become surer of yourself you start to walk the carpets, deliver the lines, portray the emotions as though that is what you are meant to be doing and soon enough it becomes a reality. Trust me even I struggle to adjust to the cameras sometimes!'

The shape swivelled back to the cameras as it said 'Florence Rose talking about her new film Greendale Getters'

Away from the spying spotlights, I felt myself shudder, the glass hands and cold eyes tickling the back of my neck as I gathered my heels and my heavy dress into the venue.

Each carafe of wine they brought round, each tray of cocaine they offered, I took. I smiled seeing each item as something I deserved, a physical token of accomplishment, of deserving, all accolades on my swollen shelf of success.

I had conquered the mountain of the self and planted the flag in my own image, clambering up the rocks from dust at the bottom. Born to become those that stare at the top as if it were art only to become one of the pioneers that make it a reality.

As a child I didn't watch TV, I memorised it, each line, each accent, was mine. Each heartbreak, each emotional earthquake I echoed. My bedtime stories were theatrical displays my parents would applaud for.

Frozen to my seat, cramp in my jaw from my stretched skin, my eyes began to water with the wait for other people's success, their irrelevant categories ran before the 3 I had been nominated for. Throughout their cliched speeches about their family, friends, and fans, I had to remind myself this would be broadcasted so I reacted dutifully and respectfully to each story, even allowing my tired eyes to water when appropriate.

As I looked into the audience, there were a few with different passion passes. I assumed they were the parents, sitting with their pride and joy in their rightful place.

I could see what their smiles really stood for 'Your success is our success'. Even vultures are vulnerable without their prey.

As the stage dwellers beat back silver tears I thought of my parents who I hadn't seen since my second film hit the carpets. I thought about my past and how I had gotten here tonight.

My mother was an artist with a half-decent portfolio and a print in the gallery, she floated in circles but left few footsteps while my father had left a few years into my childhood, unable to handle the pressure of being a dad and too committed to his passions of being an origamist.

He used to make my mother swans, dragons, and flowers. Now whenever I see a paper swan I begin to cry, which has come in handy on a set so in some way my absent dad did support my career.

 Initially, my mother hadn't wanted much from her art other than to make it. Then dad left and she realised she had wasted 10 years of her time devoting herself to people who wouldn't devote themselves back. She started spending more time in the city, always excusing her negligence with a big opportunity to make more art.

When he left and she was in the sleeping section I tried to entertain her as a distraction, to try to make her stay. I would perform in my friends' plays, I would mimic accents and deliver convincing lies to get out of trouble.

 The more theatrics I caused, the more my passion grew until I was able to pursue open roles for the adverts found for me by my Faceless, the only 'gift' that my mother got me.

 In my first on-screen role, I played Mia in a sitcom called Dollar Pingere about an aspiring artist who could only capture true beauty after witnessing a violent tragedy. I had to orchestrate train crashes and convince people to sacrifice themselves for others in order to be recognised for my worth.

I understood it for what it was, an allegory for the industry, the isolation that came with all eyes on you. Loveless, despite convincing all those who do not know you that you are worthy of love. Each opportunity to convince them you are happy, that you are everything they wish they could be. They will either be inspired by this forced narrative or ruined by it and raze your reputation.

But I am older now, no longer that peppy teenager but a pensioner in the eyes of the lens, slouched at 26 in my seat wearing my fan dress, a desperate attempt to show people I was still a relevant actress.

I am sitting at a table with shining faces who need no introduction, I know everything about them, but we have barely said more than hello. I am essentially sat alone but that is okay, I no longer need the hold of my mum or my dad. I have huge cabinets all over my penthouse full of shiny things, I do not need my forehead kissed.

During a pause between categories, I excused myself to the bathroom, sauntering instead into my VIP backroom.

Finding faces that did not belong to me staring back in the mirror I peeled each part of me off before trying to rearrange it into some sense of familiarity. A patchwork of other people, I pieced myself back together. I would not cry for my sacrifices for they were getting me where I was supposed to be.

 I would not pine for things that no longer existed. I wiped my tears and breathed deeply, retrieving a cheat sheet script out of my decolletage. One final run-through despite knowing that I was already word perfect. A quick touch up of my hair and another bump of cocaine as my Faceless tightened my dress.

It would be decided tonight if I would win, or I would lose. But being here, being under these lights, the world was already my trophy.

Names were repeated until they became what they were, meaningless. A name could only be meant when it was your own and when it was announced alone.

Dresses in red, dresses made out of glass, dresses that were made out of metal and dresses that were barely there kissed the stairs. Leather suits, plastic suits and paper suits all followed. I sat smiling, knowing my turn would be soon.

My first acting role landed me the award of best young adult on screen, the year before that I was awarded for delivering the most convincing performance. Once again I felt the camera pan to my face, its presence sudden and intimate, I offered it a look drenched in appropriate nerve and an appreciative smile.

"And the winner of the Faceless shout-outs for the Best Supporting Actress is…"

 Silence. I had heard this sort of silence a thousand times now, I felt unphased by its presence as I knew what would come out of it. Slightly unsettled by how much suspense was being built up, I shuddered and then there it was, my name, filling out the stadium, booming out to the hundreds. I collapsed into the fold of my hands for a millisecond then, I exhaled and stood, still shaking, I managed a step. I had wanted this more than I needed sunlight.

The presenter was thin and boring to look at, his features fading just as I tried to grasp them. I held his hollow gaze and filled awkward pauses with wit and joke until he eventually handed out my award, Best Supporting Actress.

Knowing my parents weren't watching, I decided to thank myself for always fighting my corner, the director for pushing me out into the ring and the fans for cheering me on, then with just ten seconds to go I spoke into the camera.

 "This is your sign to change your situation, and in doing so help others to change theirs. Find something that means as much as this passion does to me and do it earnestly"

A shattered chandelier of applause crescendoed across the auditorium, my tearfully, smiling face reflected in their half-empty, raised glasses. I bowed and strutted off stage stumbling back to my seat as I held my metal figurine high.

The night was far from over with rumours of an afterparty swirling around the room like autumn wind.

Chapter Eight
John

With my mind blank as the winter sky, I asked the passion plaque what I wanted to do. Something new, 'Museum'.

I struggled through the city to the destination of all inspiration for creators like me, The Museum of Now.

Chiselled and golden, an opulent prism of optimism, a beacon to us all that if we want it enough then we too can be part of its walls. Both a lighthouse of possibility and a beautiful, looming tower of perpetual pressure, its motto engraved in platinum on the front 'Spectateur et voilut out vigilate at vollo velle' - join us and be watched or watch us live on without you. Only by witnessing greatness could you ever get a shot at being it.

This is where my people are, engrossed in who they could be, staring up at what became. A ceiling higher than hope and walls flooded with faces, success has few ancestors, and they all reside here. I scan my passion plaque and after dutiful consideration, the glass screens slide open for me, permitting me access to gawk at other people's achievements.

Being surrounded by framed success allowed for potential whereas being at parties and drinking at Jada's penthouse felt like a competition, trying to struggle for the space to step into your own life. Here miles of minds and their medallions shimmer in glass cages, beyond my reach yet still beckoning to me.

Icons heralding inspiration, each face with a knowing smile that they had made it and whoever was receiving them was still trying to. Poetry about self-identity and stories lending a hand into escapism, songs that showed the soul of the musician and instruments still stained with the showmanship of its wielder.

 A labyrinth of masterminds, all leading us forward. A fortress of fortune full of relics and antiques, drawings, and music. Flickering videos of projected people performing their latest routines, my footpath became their stage. It seems even the very foundations are moved by what it holds.

 Captivating corridors dressed in doodles of named icons and real pieces of litter crafted together to create bins avenued the hallways. I wanted to be all over this museum but for now, I was looking for one specific room, hidden down in the word wing.

'There is still motion in periods of inertia, there is a heartbeat when everything is still', read a quote on the wall.

'To rise and to rest in order to reset is the only path to shine as bright as the midday sun' another phrase from a fallen passage out of a random book.

Reading the rewards of other people's thinking, I question the structure of myself and why writing is my calling, why is it that I want to warp words into worlds? It was odd that there were reams of other people's words, but I had yet to find a story that resonated with my plight.

'There is freedom and fear in the future when it is down to you to define what that is', whispered another wall.

I had no future, I only ever had today and today was never enough. I slipped up over each sentence I read, tripped up by my inner torment that I should be writing these words whilst knowing I would never be able to.

I cannot fill myself with the voices of others and hope they will teach me how to speak. I could hear the eclipse over my rising sun begin to shift into place. Feeling both disappointed in my duty to myself yet determined not to cave, I marched on to the room I was here for.

My favourite room in the entire museum was a mostly empty one. Buried deep in the heart of the word wing, it stayed silent, occupied with just a chair, a desk, a writing pot, a pile of paper and a mirror, allowing your face to join those on the wall, reminding you of your own potential to hang.

For a passion price, you could book the room out for two hours and it was almost guaranteed the walls would breathe some fair fortune on you, an unseen masterpiece flowing from your fingertips.

I book myself in and watch as the door slowly closes, I am the only person in existence now. It is only me who I have to defeat. It is up to me to rebuild the world with the words in my head, but the blank pages always fill me with dread. Pen to paper, heart to hand, I tried to give it my all.

I would sit here all night until the pen began to flow from left to write.

Chapter Nine
Jill

Seed scars sat on the surface of my skin as I pulled more grains from my scalp and nibbled them from my fingernails.

I had run out of capsules for the Famia a day or two ago but couldn't leave to get more. I sat in front of the TV as I gnawed at what was left. It had been another week and my skin had been starved of touch, of Mark.

How I craved to be kicked accidentally or bumped into by a stranger just to feel something. I couldn't go outside even if I wanted to, the fear of danger outweighed the want of touch. I was kept captive by my own creation, but no feeling would end its hold.

Sat on the sofa, I could hear the birds happily chirping, I had made sure to count them, grateful I could call them company.

My face felt like a smudge as I longed for more sound, sick of staring at my own reflection for some form of connection. As the birds weaved their world I switched mine off, tuning into strangers to steal some semblance of unity.

As lovers intertwined themselves before me I stole their arms and wrapped them around my waist. In my mind Mark was warm, he engulfed me, his head resting upon mine, but soon our skin fell silent through lack of memory.

Once, we had sung together and now I longed for whispers. I tried to imagine the solid shape of his silhouette, the signature scent of his sweat, and the size of his hands as he held mine.

Our love was like bird seeds, we could have been something beautiful if handled correctly, watered, and left in sunlight, with patient encouragement as it began to blossom but instead, it was consumed whole and left to thrive in the dark. So the dark is where I stayed, pretending his voice was just one echo away from mine.

More time passed, more birds were counted, more strangers confessing true love to each other. The key in the door startled me from an eyes half shut slumber.

I switched the TV off and waltzed into his arms, waiting for him to sprinkle his day over me so I could pick at his words like precious jewels, but he stayed silent.

Sweat stuck to his skin like a frown on a forehead, and his heavy arms dropped to his side. He lightly pulled me off and walked into the kitchen. Unsettled by his silence, I stepped into a state of inertia hiding from rumbling thunder, legs tense as though the ground beneath me was beginning to crack.

I could hear him banging cupboards and fists into counters, a hurricane in the corner of the house.

"Mark, how have you been, how were the projects?", I whispered.

His heavy footsteps and frustrated fists responded, an angered drum singing to a broken beat.

"How has your time been my love?", I asked.

He huffed, a bitter laugh leaving his frozen body.

"Yeah, it was great Jill, where's the famia?"

"We're out of capsules for it"

"What?"

"We've run out..."

Another bitter burn of laughter oozed off his tongue, verging on venomous, the ice within me avalanches throughout my body. I stood as a statuesque soldier who had lost their sword and shield, trying not to collapse with the weight of defeat.

"You haven't got any more capsules? You are so useless. You are so exhausting, look at you. Look at you. Find a mirror and stand in it. What do you see? You're an echo of a person Jill."

"I am sorry, I didn't realise until you were gone otherwise I would have said. I'm really sorry, you know the shop will be open."

"How would you know Jill? God, I leave you and I leave you and still, you refuse to stand alone. Who are you? You sit and you watch, you watch and you sit. What kind of life is that?"

"Mark I know you aren't really angry at me, I know it's the projects, what happened, where have you been?"

"You don't know anything. You sit and you rot, you are a waste of resources. I don't even want to look at you."

Burning liquid flew into my chest, tears welled in my eyes. I was back in the building I had vowed to turn away from all those years ago.

"I get scared."

"Ah so you sit, rot and get scared? Why do you want to live like that Jill?"

He was staring at me now, a visual duel between us where I would hand him my joust and let him stab me with it for the sake of silence.

"It keeps me safe, you know it does, and that is what I want."

"I keep you safe Jill, I keep you alive, look at this", pointing to a pile of seed crumbs scattered across the carpet. "You would be dead without me and what recognition do I get for that? A wife whose skin doesn't even want to be a part of her, a wife who only cares for birds and fiction."

"That is who you married", I wept.

He huffed again, pushing past me, his shoulder knocking into mine and sending me a step back, I ached for more of this attention, but I knew this wasn't right.

I heard the door slam but still I stood, shaking. Mark had snapped before but it was always a bruise over a broken bone, he always came back, refusing to leave me on my own.

I knew he wanted me to follow him, to leave the house but I couldn't. I wanted to be better for him but to deliver this meant danger. The garden was the only slice of the outside I could stand in, fortified by the fences that Mark had built, I could be safe.

I could stick my head out into the front garden, but I rarely did due to the fear of what might be lurking. I wanted to follow him, but I couldn't go outside.

I wrapped a blanket around myself and sank back into the sofa, swallowing my show in big gulping sobs.

He returned a few hours later wearing the same shroud of silence, a thin shield between him and I. He stormed into the kitchen pushing the capsule into the famia, before waiting whilst it made what he wanted.

He came with a beer and cheesy chips, avoiding eye contact with me as he was swallowed by the realm of the upstairs.

I made my bed on the sofa and after eating the remainder of my nails, I fell asleep.

When I rose, he was gone.

Chapter Ten
Florence

The trickle of champagne towers flowing, the sharp click of heels and shuffle of leather loathers, these were the sound of a successful party. A large group congregated in front of a larger silver head mounted at the top of the wall. They were all pulling faces and posing with drinks for the cameras.

Some people were murmuring about when other celebrities would be arriving, with a rumoured performance from Jada on its way.

Of course, when the Faceless opened the doors for me, my shimmering structure was met with a thunderstorm of applause.

People swarmed to me, I had brought the fireworks to the night sky, and the sound of their interest and intrigue became my stage as I told them all about the behind the scenes and got dangerously drunk on personalised bottles of champagne.

But it was nothing compared to when Jada arrives. Everyone screams when Jada arrives, falling over each other to be able to stand in her presence, as if just to be near a beacon was to be part of their light.

We all danced to her voice, our bodies a force of celebration, a force of gratitude for her being there. With the spotlight off me, I felt the sick fizz in my throat.

In the crowded loo, I steal a few moments to find myself, to pull myself out of the noise, practising gratitude for my own presence to be granted access to such a wonderful place tonight.

My first role saw my name in lights, and my second role just served to brighten them. I was everywhere. I was Victoria, the ghost that haunted Blackwood manor convincing a living soul that I was his, slowly tormenting him to madness.

I was ditzy Lily, a bookstore owner wooed by a ventriloquist who convinced me to be his loving puppet in a 12-part TV show called 'Puppet Love'.

At first, when I took a bow I felt I owed it to the Faceless. They understood that others wanted me to win, they had understood that I wanted these roles and thus were worthy of them.

I was always brought back up by those who stood in the dark applauding me, a sea of silhouetted faces and an ocean of flashing lights. I was not just a star but the whole night sky

There was a knock and a grunt from outside of my cubicle.

"If you're in there doing drugs because you don't want to share, don't worry most people have got their own but some of us actually need to go."

I wiped away my tears of pride and opened the door with a smile only to be met with a look of disgust on a younger actress' face

"Makes sense it would be you who would still be in there."

I didn't know who this woman was and shuddered as I left the bubbling room, missing the shroud of anonymity. It fell back upon me when the winner of the lead actress arrived, carried in by her Faceless.

She was covered in diamonds, rubies, and emeralds. Everyone had to stay a foot away from her throughout the night, as she shimmered and smiled, sauntering to the centre of the room so everyone could watch her dance, her head held aloft, straining her neck in the process as she waltzed with her own shadow. I rolled my eyes.

No one cares about the supporting actress when the lead is in the way. I took a couple of champagnes from the diminishing tower and went up to the balcony to stare at the city.

Jada was already up there, standing alone, enjoying her final sips of a sapphire margarita.

I coughed on my approach so as to not startle her. I noticed she had taken her shoes off and loosened the fastenings of her dress a little. She took another sip and turned around, smiling when she recognised me.

"Hey Flo, I always forget how big these galas are. You sing a sold-out show, and it feels as if you are sharing your soul with your friends, whereas here you sing and you feel you are being stared at and compared to."

Nodding whilst swallowing champagne, I silently understood what she meant. I felt as though I had been dissected and feasted upon, as though I were dead, and everybody here merely flies.

"I am just here to compare dresses and catch up with friends but yes it does feel as though we are part of some exhibit."

She smiled, "The city is so silent, why is it so silent? Are we the only people that exist? Was this world made just for us? Look at it, I can fit it all in my palm."

She laughed as she lowered her hand to make it appear as though she was holding the landscape right there in her outstretched fingers.

"The world is mine."

Giving her the second glass of champagne, I had commandeered I said, "Well the Faceless have made it so."

"Hmm I don't think so, I think we did this, we are our own creations, and our success is our song."

"Why did you get into this, why did you want to sing?"

She answered instantly "Because I do. How about you?"

"I do it for the people I get to be, the roles I play. To be someone else for a while", I replied. I couldn't help but think this sounded a little too rehearsed in my head.

She laughed awkwardly before saying "And you do that so well!"

I let the silence fall between us, it wasn't a bulwark, it was an understanding, a quiet nod that said she saw me. I felt the burn of sick again.

"Do you have any painless pills?"

She handed me two from her purse before saying "Shall we go back to the dancing now?" and downed her last sip of champagne.

Chapter Eleven
Mark

Use and used. I am used to being used, it makes me feel useful. But then I realise what I have been used for and is all useless and when I come home I am surrounded by more uselessness.

I am married to a woman who wants nothing more but for me to be me, but I cannot be me for her anymore, I have to be me for me.

Of course, she loves me, and I know I care about her but there is more to my life than hers and I can't watch her starve herself from the sun anymore.

I hunger for more after eating, whilst she is happy having nothing. My previous time at the projects had seen us producing another bridge, we had tried to do it differently this time as one of the women suggested it should be made out of steel instead of concrete to increase durability.

She then used her skills to carve intricate art into its beams, showing us how we could do the same. I had carved a bird, determined to persuade Jill out of the house so I could show her.

At the end of the week, once the bridge had been up for 5 days, the Faceless took it down. Everyone blamed the woman, telling her steel had been too expensive, our carving had been a waste of time and as they hadn't been authentically passionate about it, the Faceless had scrapped it all, so she did not return.

I once enjoyed walking through the city as a source of inspiration. Now I walk through with a bitter burn of resentment imprisoning my imagination.

This begins to bubble when I stumble past the Liatrium, a building I had produced blueprints for, before submitting them to the Faceless to get passion points to pursue their project. It was rejected, my blueprints burned, and another bridge was requested instead.

I stand small beneath it, both impressed and intimidated, by this beacon of beauty. Its wide arches and stoic columns, its open spaces, and welcoming steps.

Standing on them, I look at the carvings, the limestone swirls and shapes, the marble detailing, the days it would have taken me and my mates, and the glory I would have felt stepping back from securing the last brick.

I realise some of the stones used were ones we had produced, under the guise that they had been for a bird bath in the local park. We were never told, never celebrated, never credited. How ironic that an institute of inspiration could cause so much resentment.

Some of what we had produced still stood. There was a statue of a late artist we had carved standing in the park, a bridge across a stream in another, and a few of the town benches I had assembled myself. I had carved each creation with the same want, so it didn't make sense that not all of them were approved.

The Museum of Now, another Faceless creation, in the style of French Baroque, modernism and opulence, I could have done that. It would have taken me longer, and I would have needed a team, but I could have carved those arches, could have mapped out those corridors, understanding I would never walk through them, I could have been part of history but I have been erased of even having the chance.

Then I walked past one of the bridges that had taken us a while, it was made out of glass and had intricate arches and watch towers just for show. Now it was on the floor, collapsed into a thousand shards of what could have been, the bricks from the towers resting on their uncomfortable beds of defeat.

I grabbed two of the bricks and brazenly stormed back to the Liatrium. Throwing them into the windows and applauding whilst they shattered, all the while knowing they would be replaced tomorrow.

Brushing the brick crumbs off my palm I was still stumbling toward the direction of the projects until I felt the city-state change before me. An empty concrete corridor appeared. It was framed by non-descript establishments, a generic clothes shop, a Faceless barber and a restaurant.

But it was a bar that beckoned to me, brightly lit with wide, open windows full of smiling strangers and music. I observed its insides as though recalling a distant memory: the bitter smell of hops and the sweet sound of male laughter, the banging of glass on wooden tables. I stepped in, a beer would clean my bitter mind, so I just went for one.

This is how it began. I promise you I tried to push through, tried to get back to the projects but I always found the bar. I always stayed for one and ended up having four. I would then stumble past the Liatrium, throwing a brick or two at it, kicking the door and crying on the steps before finding myself stumbling into a different bar instead of finding a home.

I made friends with the residents, the guys who desired to drink, and the women who always ordered a bottle of wine each. I was appreciated every time I walked in. We wouldn't talk about much, but that didn't matter, nobody in there wanted to do much talking.

In the end, each street I passed down was littered with wine stains and shimmering shards of broken glass. Each bar is a room full of both silence and shouters, some angry, some sad, some indifferent, some smiling but rarely with happiness. I was no longer able to differentiate between a whispered sentence and the start of a fight.

If there was no violence, lips were greeting each other, hands on hips and under tables, down trousers, and up skirts. Every action was an act of passion. If you had blood on your knuckles or lipstick on your neck you were a champion.

After a while, on some darker days, the silence returned, the harrowing images of dreams destroyed haunted my head. Even the drink couldn't drown it out.

The smiling faces all became snarling teeth with threatening eyes. Each face a constant reminder that there is a future, but it does not necessarily belong to you. I had to drink myself into dullness to not take them up on their apparent attacks.

Until I wasn't able to swallow down the silence and strangled a man to get him to stop staring at me. His friend eventually pulled me off him to the crowds' dismay. He threw me into a corner, holding me by the neck.

"We can all be heroes mate, we can all bring people to a deserving death. I can do that to you if I ever see your hands anywhere other than to yourself again. I've been watching you for a while and I actually pity you."

I spluttered as his grip loosened.

 "I've been where you are, you need something better now. Take this with your drinks and it will change your life, everyone in here is on them by now."

He stuck a square tab on my tongue that slowly dissolved. "Don't worry mate it will all start to taste like home now."

I turned to everyone in the room, some close by were looking, reassuringly nodding whilst all others were too deep down into their drink and drugs to look at me. I had never considered taking drugs before. Most people did, most people wanted them, and even their plaques would tell them to pursue them from time to time, like a treat, a reward for getting through another day.

Didn't I deserve this? Hadn't I got through many days others would not have woken for? Did I not try? I did what I wanted, and this was now another of those things. My whole existence was belittled and stymied, by these so-called saviours. Everyone on them was happy. So I took it, and I haven't looked back since.

Dissolving my dreams into my drinks and swallowing them whole. Injecting friends into my fingertips and between my toes. An instant feeling of warmth, the feeling of being known.

Syringes of liquid survival passed between friends, when some refuted this offer other firsts were thrown, and some weary cheers were chucked around as fingers met throats and eyes closed. Pinhole vision, every stranger is stood in a spotlight, a smile, or a snarl each expression entertained before the fall.

The stars are sparkling for you, you bow and cheer, each step, now your stage, everyone is the man in here.

Chapter Twelve
John

Hours spent sacrificing the embrace of the Sun sat in the cruel kiss of darkness, I had done it. The pile of paper in front of me was decorated with genius.

These would be the words that would return the books to the Liatrium, instead of the dusty corner they dwelled in, these were the words that would bring my readers back to me. Once nothing, I wrote myself back into the world and became everything. I am everything. I have these books, I have my words, and my passion is enough, I have proven that. I chose to try and it paid off.

Writing the closing paragraphs, 'With my tongue I carve worldly creations for you to drown in, I rise and begin like the waves to the shore I persevere and rise one more, like the soot and the ash I am evidence of what once was, your watching eyes a perpetual applause'. I could feel myself running back into my arms. Once typed, the pages appeared before me printed and piled in the order they needed to be in.

My paper progress, my proof of passion, meant my wants were worth something. A slice of my soul that showed I was deserving of a place in the present. I went to the submission section in the Museum.

A Faceless took my paper and a circular pit appeared in front of me perfectly shaped to the mould of my head.

Although the paper could be scanned for passion, my mind had to fit the mould of the words in order to make sure that my thoughts matched the world on the pages.

With the paper in the slot, I closed my eyes and thought about all I had written, all born through passion, passion, passion.

The hum of the scanner stopped and I lifted my head knowing I had done enough to make a difference. The Faceless would see this was what I wanted, these were words born from total self-belief. I left knowing I would see those words again, but they would be bound in leather, and they would be beautiful.

I allowed myself a celebratory detour to the detox bar. Filled with the regulars, an unfamiliar face like mine caused some stirs, some blank stares and paused conversations as they assessed if I were one of them or a straggler from the street, then someone shouted "John!" and conversation flowed again.

I recognised Jada through her disguise instantly. She was wearing a bobbed, blonde wig, a large prosthetic nose and a tattoo on her chiselled stomach but her essence was one I could recall blindfolded and deaf.

It had been 6 months since her party, 6 months since I had last heard from her. It was good to see her in the flesh again, a face made more radiant by the memories our minds shared.

"Oh my god, John I cannot believe you are here! I was just showing the guys some of my old stomps."

The guys were not the usual Faceless frames that celebrities stuck by but were actually real people, her stoic army of three bodyguards, both shielding her and framing her in a way that kept her in a permanent spotlight. Imagine being that powerful that people actually want to protect you.

"How's it going?"

"Actually, I just submitted some papers."

"Benny get my boy a sapphire strength."

"Your famia does that?"

"It does everything, but I like it old style, authentic, really, my bodyguard Benny makes it proper."

'Thanks", I said as he handed me a vibrant blue liquid punctuated by flecks of gold. It tasted of the earth and made me feel as though I had swallowed the sun.

"So what was it about? The paper you submitted. I remember you always writing something, quoting sentences like you were reciting the alphabet."

"Nothing really, it'll probably get rejected, I forced myself to do it, I just needed to get some words down."

"Don't do yourself down like that, have you ever heard me say something like that about one of my songs? Come on, what was it about?"

"It's called 'Maternal Instincts'. Envision a world where violence is wrong, and some people are in place to prevent it called Vestigers. One of the vestigers is trying to prove her position and gets the opportunity when the town's singer is brought to her death, only to see how the story spirals and how her mother may be involved. It's different I know but I thought maybe being different would create change."

"I can see the blurb now, 'Maternal Instincts a gripping tale of perseverance, familial bond, and unyielding determination in the face of adversity'."

"You actually inspired it, at the party stopping that fight. I have never seen somebody do that before."

"I don't want anyone dying on my property whether they deserve to or not. That sounds like a really fun concept John. 'Vestiger?' Funny word. And just death, not deserving death, so in this world is it wrong to bring the end to somebody's life?"

"Yeah, in this world it would be wrong to want to do that. I mean I think it is odd in real life, but I understand the sport behind its."

Only her body answered this with a slight shudder, her smile dropping slightly.

"Another sapphire strength?'"

She nodded.

"A toast. To good friends, to sad songs and to happy endings."

We all cheered before I downed my drink.

A few more toasts later Jada told me she was proud of me. Both an icon and an idol, 12-time award-winning artist was proud of me. I didn't have to ask her what she was up to, everyone already knew.

Her life broadcasted on the Basi, the countdown to her next song release a constant cause for celebration.

"No really, like you were a ghost for years but here you are still kicking, really making life your own. John, I always had faith, you're like me! Look we are the same, I have my bodyguards you have yourself, and that is enough."

"'Is it?"

"What do you mean? If you're passionate it's enough John don't be ridiculous", she laughed.

"Yeah I know."

"You're a tour de force, I am a tour de force. But all tour de forces will face obstacles, it is how you face them that matters. Do not fear if the Faceless don't push this through, it is the journey that matters."

I nodded not wanting to entertain the idea that the Faceless may reject yet another of my word submissions.

There is nothing sparkly about mundanity, or monotony; there is only passion, and without it you are nothing.

Chapter Thirteen
Will

The hands of the children held on to me, and I took their gaze with me as I watched the world. Each time I returned home, struggling with how to help them. I started to pick all the dishevelled literature up from the shelves and read ancient worlds that had heralded children as the future.

I read about the structure of societies that flowed in harmony. I learned that the origins of passion had come from the word pain, meaning to suffer, and I finally felt the truth in my stomach.

Despite the smile on my face, I had been suffering. Alone for years in my parent's absence, left to fill the estate with friends who could now not recall my name and the Faceless had allowed this.

I understood now that the Faceless had deceived people into believing they could pursue the demands of their desires, despite doing so to their own detriment.

At first, people believed they were deities. If they wanted it they simply had to ask, and it would be theirs. Eventually, the gluttony of self and the gorging on one's own future would only leave them unsatiated and dissatisfied.

They could eat all they wanted but would end up an unhealthy weight and if they wanted to lose it they would have to do stuff they didn't want to do. They would want to fall in love but wouldn't want the heartbreak, they wanted to do well but didn't realise what this truly meant and got annoyed when what they wanted wasn't bestowed upon them.

So the Faceless adapted, realising they had upset their masters and wanted to do better for them. They let them be lazy, then let them stay in painful places and told them it was love, they told them they were good enough because it is what they wanted to hear.

They had taught those who believed they were good that they were in fact good when in reality they were talentless. Why do we place such people on pedestals?

Talent is not being able to hold a note, or write a moving poem, talent comes in the form of saviours, people who are truly successful, care for others and want to develop a better sense of those around them.

In a world of endless possibilities, it is so much more reassuring to take the easiest route. In a world where you can be what you want, who would choose to be good?

Had I been good? What does good mean when there is no gauge of goodness or badness, just different levels of worth. I had felt good throwing the parties, drinking until it all came up and drugging myself out of this celestial plane, but it hadn't done good, it hadn't felt good in the abandoned aftermath.

As I read on, I began to understand. I set about destroying the family of Faceless that haunted the halls of my humanity, melting them down in a fire I made them create. Out of the 20 that I had, I kept one so I could learn as much as I could from it.

I thought back to the passion plaque, a more contemporary version of the upside-down washing machine my parents would stick their heads into as it blinded them with white space, a gap their heads would fill with what they truly wanted.

I remember the hollow stare behind my father's eyes as his brain was scanned for passion, for any evidence of creative thought, and my mother's heavy breathing as the machine began to whir at an alarming rate as it spiralled around her skull.

Whatever filled the gap determined how many passion points they were worthy of, the more creative, the more passion points. It determined how worthy they were to the world... not to themselves.

How fortunate they both were, how much they wasted their potential wondering if they had any. Why hadn't the estate been enough for them? Where were they now?

I felt small hands on my shoulder and cold eyes, watching me through my warm windows. I thought of all the food I had ordered from the Faceless just so I could watch it rot and I began to choke on my tears, knowing that the easy flow of their presence was a privilege.

You believe you have greatness bestowed on you, just because you want it? You are promised the possibility of the Basi, your name announced to strangers, your face shared across the city. You believe you have a right to be known not caring what you are known for because you know it will be for the good. You are born with a name, you should spend your life trying to live up to it.

The utter removal of your own individual initiative, the reliance on some external being to tell you what you wanted, the lack of trust within yourself to find what it was. The need to be told you are great, some constant form of validation, from something that has never seen your face.

Imagine a world instead where you can do good and feel good, one where you can gain the respect and appreciation of your peers without selling your soul to be on the Basi for a while before being toppled by the next greater than.

We don't want to be greedy, we want to be great but true greatness cannot be harnessed when there is guilt. When we are driven by desire we are fuelled by self-interest, where we want to be recognised by our peers for who we are, where we want to refine our skills rather than be given them.

The more I read the more I thought, pacing the halls and staring into the dark corners of my mind. How could I stop this pain, how could I save so many from suffering?

Then one day it was clear, sitting in the green library in the far west wing of the main house I learned a new word 'work'.

 I learned that it meant to be fulfilled, improving yourself and sharpening your skills whilst contributing to the community. I read this and knew I had started a war.

Chapter Fourteen

Jill

Loneliness was something I had made friends with, something I sat with. I did not want to sit alone but I understood why I did. It was the happiness I found in the hollow of my head that kept the smile on my face. Sadness was too closely associated with silence but there was always so much sound.

Even when the sleeping section was quiet, especially with Mark gone, there were the birds, the wind, the TV, and occasionally a face walking across the street before vanishing. But there was no one to make me laugh, make me smile, make me wonder.

I relied on faraway faces and digital deals to drag a sound out of me. I always had the birds, but they just reminded me of how alone I was in this life, and they too left at sunset.

I think back to where I was before, the same place just with different walls, when I was much smaller and to breathe too loud was a deserved death to yourself.

I had once lived with my two sisters, Grace, and Emily, in a sleeping section much smaller than this, two bedrooms, a lounge and a diner. One of the bedrooms was ours, then the rest of the building belonged to the Voice.

 I think Grace was 6, Emily was 9 and at this point, I may have been 14. We didn't celebrate or even know when our birthdays were, but I knew I was the eldest. I was the responsible one.

In the mornings, when the Voice was still asleep, my sisters and I would count the birds. It was Grace's idea and as the youngest we let her get her way. She always looked out for the bluebirds, Emily would sit with us for a while before watching her favourite TV show quietly in the lounge.

It was our lucky morning routine, stealing glimpses of freedom in flight, imagining what we would do and where we would go if we were those birds. Always wondering why they had chosen our garden of all others to sing in. When we heard the Voice stir we would run back upstairs, forcing ourselves into a false sleep to avoid their glare and relentless demands.

They would shake us awake, berating us for sleeping in. Refusing to get a Faceless, it was us that had to prepare their food with the few remaining ingredients, to organise the immaculate rooms and to sit quietly in the Voice's presence. We had to be of use to them or we'd be abused.

On some days the Voice would vanish, and the building heaved with happiness, a relieved sigh perceptibly leaving the bones of its brick. We would have to wait for the silence to collect like dust before using it to our advantage. There were times when this would happen. The silence settled like snow, soft enough to tread on instead of designed to slip you up like ice, and we would leave.

We would walk outside to feel the city shift and swirl, until our grey scenery, a place that perpetually rained, became a golden square of sea, sand and sun. Emily had always watched shows on waves and sand so naturally we would be transported to the beach.

It was always warm, our skin always kissed by the sun, as we squealed, full of noise and laughter whilst being completely at peace. Waves would hit the sand with no force, just two lovers reuniting, a fleeting embrace.

Seagulls would laugh amongst themselves as they ruled the world's ceiling whilst my sisters and I would splash around in the shallows, or dance on the shore, before sharing salty chips as we shivered ourselves dry in the setting sun.

This place made peace feel possible, it meant that we could go on outside our world of four walls. We did this a few times, the same beach, the same seagulls. Grace and Emily always watched the other children do tricks and tried to copy them, always ketchup for Grace on one side and mayonnaise on the other for Emily and me, when we shared our chips.

Always hushed voices after I had eventually wrangled them back to the sleeping section, always a relief and a nervous chuckle when we arrived, and the Voice was not yet back.

We would go to the woods to see the birds up close, offering handfuls of birdseed. I would tell an elated Grace to stay still, as Emily sulked that it was too cold in the woods for her, complaining that we should probably get back. I hushed her, reassuring her that we wouldn't be too long. She started sword-fighting a distant tree whilst Grace spread her outstretched palms to hungry birds.

 A blue bird flittered down to her palm and pecked. She offered a delighted bubble of laughter which scared the bird away. I tried but none came to me, so we poured a pile of seeds into a busy bird section of the woods and watched as they swarmed down. The brown carpet came alive with a kaleidoscopic explosion of colour, even Emily wandered over to take a look, quietly impressed at the display.

We shifted between the beach and the woods when we could, stealing our childhood wherever possible. Cleaning our hands and washing our mouths before the Voice returned, scrubbing away at any evidence of our existence as we got on with the list they had left us to get through in their absence.

When the Voice was gone we always had the day that children are supposed to have, sun, sand and too many salty chips. Then I took it too far.

 Grace had never properly swum before and although she enjoyed paddling she was scared of the waves so she built sandcastles, whilst Emily was always busy trying to perfect her cartwheels or plucking up the confidence to ask the other children if she could be involved in what they were doing.

 I could swim slowly and only after mimicking a few others I saw in the water and on TV, I wanted to get better so I told Emily to watch Grace as I paddled out.

I was floating, not too far from shore, watching the sky and smiling at the circling seagulls, as the waves washed over me.

My heavy legs beat down the water around me as my arms lifted me up and over. I was calm as some water got up my nose or went over my head, always finding my way back up.

I didn't realise how long I had been doing this until the distant shrill scream of a desperate child deafened my ears, taken aback I was toppled over by a larger wave, taking me deep under and into its stomach.

 I found my way up and blinked out the burning salt from my eyes, looking at the shore I could make out Emily, skinny and star-shaped, her hands high waving frantically. I couldn't see Grace.

Another wave took me down, panicking. I tried to push it off me, but they only pushed me further, the peace from their grip had gone and the strength rivalled the Voice's. I couldn't fight against the waves that pinned me down like a beast, dragging me into its stomach.

The Voice came down with me, fists and fingers, the gurgle of the sea mocking me, weak, pathetic, dragging me further down into its fatal farewell. It got darker and the sun was gone, feeling the sea settle over me. I was falling.

Seeing the Voice smile in my mind, I thought of my sisters, I thought of the seagulls above and kicked. My heart pushing for the surface, my fingers grasping for its, I collapsed on top of the wave. I pushed away from its grasp and fought for the shoreline, coughing up on the sand, throwing up seawater and undigested chips.

In between ugly gulps of relief and defeat, Emily grabbed me.

"Grace is gone."

But it didn't sound like that. My head still full of water, my eyes stinging from the salt.

"Jill, Grace is gone."

I coughed more, my skin stretching over my bones as I shuddered.

'Gone where?'

How could she be gone, this is what we did, we stayed on the beach, we stayed in eye-line of each other.

"You went out too far, she tried to go after you."

"No."

Cold fluid filled my throat, but I knew there was nothing else to throw up.

"No Em, she will be on the beach somewhere, was she hungry, did she say? Maybe she has gone to get chips..."

"No she's in there", she said pointing toward the sea.

"She is afraid of the waves Emily don't mess around now."

"You have to go back for her."

"She isn't in there Emily, if she was she'd be calling for us."

"She was but you didn't listen."

Then I remember a noise, a whisper that sounds like Emily could be telling the truth, but I shove it down.

I started screaming for her then aware that this scene was scaring the other children who had now turned to us.

"Emily, you stay here."

I pushed back through the waves. Only a few metres out the temperament of the water wouldn't be safe for a 6-year-old that couldn't swim. I didn't know how to search without being dragged under again.

A couple of the other kids, a few I realised were older than me, had started searching too.

We were all echoes of each other in the face of an unhearing drum. An hour passed and it was clear that Grace was gone. I stayed searching for another day or so, aware that it was hopeless but not caring, I wasn't going to let her go.

Emily and I didn't speak as the beach shifted back to the sleeping section. We never really spoke again, in fact, the only sound I heard for years was that of the Voice's who beat me until my bones broke and my clothes were red. I was to sleep in the cupboard only to come out when I was needed. I had no bed, no light, just myself and my guilt.

I had wanted her to come back more than I wanted to breathe but she had wanted to go more than I wanted her to stay. After that, I stopped wanting much, wanting peace would be enough.

These shadows of the past are reborn sporadically, a product of stagnation. Sometimes, as I sit and watch the triangular wings of the starling spread and the yellow breast of the blue tit swell with the morning song I sometimes get the scent of something, swirling in from the past.

 It comes unexpectedly, never delivered by a known face, just placed in my throat as I go to swallow. The taste of life before Mark, a bitter misery full of thunder and salt. The taste of dark days and warm December, an unsettling storm brewing in the skies, full of lightning that never strikes. Purple skin and swollen eyes, full of sore throats and desperate cries.

In Grace's absence, when I was eventually let out of the cupboard, I made it my duty to count the birds for her, to sit in the window each morning and watch. One day the Voice called me in, they had something they needed me to do and stupidly I stood still, still counting the birds for a second longer than allowed. The Voice's hand grabbed me and tied me down to the kitchen chair.

"You want to stay there too long? Stay there forever. You want something to watch instead of listening to me? I'll give you something to watch."

They made me watch as they cut the tree down. Emily sobbed in the corner as I was denied the right to cry. There was no more song for years after that, if I looked outside the hand was raised.

For years since Grace drowned, since I let Grace drown, I obeyed the rules and stayed indoors, in sight doing what I could to make things right. Approaching adulthood, I decided it was time to do as she had done and leave.

At first, I would sit in the local park, seeing the birds again, always returning after an hour or two, to continue with my tasks. Spending hours with my head in the clouds and finding happiness in their embrace. I would return to this park when I made the Voice drinks knowing how to make them sleep a little while longer. Eventually, there was another voice that entered my life.

This one was softer, like quiet rainfall at the start of autumn. We would spend what time we could together, I would tell him about the birds I was watching, he would tell me about stuff he had built.

He was confused when I had to rush off even though we had spoken a few times now, I always lied and told him there was something I had to finish or start. He never asked what or pried into it too much and I appreciated that. His skin was golden, his hair the brown of the branches, I clung to his arms which were broad like trunks and his smile was warm like the summer. Mark. My Mark.

Over the moments we threaded together, our romance became a remedy, a revolution in our kiss. His skin on mine meant safety, its meant I would survive. It was always this park, our park. The birds became ours, this small plot of green was a promise of eternity.

But one day my time with the sky and the love of my life had gone on too long and when I got back the Voice was gone. I couldn't hide, I just had to wait for the pain, numbing the noise in my brain that buzzed with apprehension, it finally came, as did the locks, trapped in my room, an island.

The Voice cut the trees down in the local park and each day the hand would deliver plucked wings from the birds I had once watched, presenting their corpses to me piece by piece. I was to live alone until each bird in that park had been delivered. I was never told how they did it, just shown it was my fault.

The last time I went outside was to see the despair of the greenery, the shrinking shrubberies and broken branches, the wooden remains of all I had loved. I escaped and found Mark, sick as the city shifted, knowing it would be the last time I needed to leave as I settled in with him.

The Voice was only human in appearance, a figure of thunder, a volatile vessel of violence and resentment, they were never angry at me, just at themselves for failing. It wasn't kind, or interesting, it wasn't intelligent or caring. It was cruel and bitter and cold, unable to accept that it had wasted its own will wanting to be angry because it was the only thing it was good at.

Although they are gone, their legacy lives on within me, I cannot leave, I see the Birds and Grace flying with them, I watch the waves and Emily forgives me. I do not deserve to leave.

Chapter Fifteen

Will

In childhood I was different. I didn't understand the Faceless, I didn't understand how I benefitted from their existence, and I didn't particularly care for them. I was my own robot. I would present pieces of production I was proud of to my parents, a little piece of art, and food I had created from plasticine.

I would run with the wind and try to beat its speed, always striving for better, only satisfied if I told myself so, not needing a robot to do it for me. I knew even at the age of 5 that every action had to be justifiable, a way of achieving something.

I would always try to outdo myself, to see my mother smile or make my father laugh. They told me I didn't need to clean up any mess I made as the Faceless would sort it, I didn't need to question why there was no food in, the Faceless would sort it, I didn't need to build a den in the woodlands as the

Faceless would do that. I didn't need to do anything the Faceless would do.

Even in my youth, their existence unsettled me, this looming chunk of metal, with no thoughts of its own but living more of a life than me.

I taught myself to avoid them where possible, sequestering myself in my father's study to read his books. I enjoyed lingering in my parent's many book rooms, getting paper cuts and sucking the blood as I reached new worlds and learned new words.

I would then try to impress my parents with this knowledge, trying to share it with my friends to see them smile, only to feel anger when they rolled their eyes.

"Why would you even bother doing that?"

"Yeah I get my Faceless to read to me but for the most part, I watch TV."

When I received my Faceless, I hid it away. Instead of it telling me I was good at something I would teach myself to actually be good at it.

For my mother's birthday I mastered an origami rose bouquet. She smiled and thanked me, praising my efforts and telling me I was a natural.

I wasn't a natural, nobody can be a natural. She didn't appreciate the effort I had put into each perfect fold. The excuse we offer to people who have no drive, 'Oh don't worry you aren't a natural', was not one I wanted to have linger.

Nothing comes naturally, everything has to be proved into existence, if you are not productive you are wasting life.

I knew that to be good you had to be focused, you had to change other people's minds, convincing them that you were good, not just thinking it.

Anything that could not be used to achieve justification for existence, was not worth doing, a TV show would be turned off by my parents before I even entered the room. They were lazy, they spent passion points they earned on liquid they enjoyed for 10 minutes whilst talking to friends about some other arbitrary thing they were pursuing to fill their day, none of it seemingly fulfilling.

Each sleep, a nightmare would enter my mind, I would be lying in bed, consuming some mindless digital drivel, crisp crumbs falling onto my overflowing rolls of skin as I scrolled through my phone watching people with better lives, productive lives, seem to thrive. Instead of resenting them for its, I judged them. My nightmare-self sat watching, thinking 'why did they want to be doing all that when it was fine for them to just sit?'

I couldn't escape. The more productive I tried to be the more ostracised I became and there is no life in being alone. As the years passed I used the Faceless, I stopped trying to live the life I had wanted as it seemed nobody else wanted it.

My youthful search for meaning, for justification for my life had proved fruitless. Instead of lamenting I gave in, hosting the parties to pretend I was happy, to feel some semblance of livelihood surrounded by others with beating hearts and creative thoughts. I knew that maintaining connections was the only way to survive.

For a while I still ran, still produced art for my parents until I realised that although I thought I was good it would not be determined as so unless the Faceless did, so I stopped trying.

Now, sitting in the green book room, I pondered the existence of the Faceless, and how they had come to be here.

Removing it from its cupboard I asked it what its purpose was.

"To aid you with getting what you want. To make you feel good about yourself."

"Why were you made?"

"To aid you with getting what you want. To make you feel good about yourself."

Useless thing. I kicked it out of frustration and shoved it back into its cupboard.

It had been a distant ancestor of mine who had invented the Faceless. She knew why she had done it but now they were here, people accepted them without question.

I looked back in the books for answers. After days of scouring for a scent of what had come before it felt like all was lost to silence until I found a small book, falling in on itself, shoved behind a bunch of others. It was called Volo and it contained the story of what once was.

The book began like this:

This is a re-telling based off of word-of-mouth stories. All actual records of this time were destroyed. This is all we think we know of the time.

The world was at war, driven by the desperation of the people who were not getting what they wanted, sickened by those who seamlessly won at what they wanted. Widespread devastation, mass death and destruction reigned as civilisations shattered. Once a vibrant metropolis now red and brown wastelands.

Small socks and shoes, bloodied and burning, strewn on the side of the street, corpses rotting slowly, bones appearing through dress clothes.

Siren screams of parents finding their dead children and loved ones losing loved ones, pierced the sky. Murder, bloodshed and brutality had all become normality.

The tug of tyres on the ashy ground only tired when resources for both sides were diminished, when families had been wiped out and only individuals remained, guns were placed down.

Too tired to rebuild what once was glorious, too hungry to care for the victims, too emotional to express, humankind was an arrow string away from extinction.

Ava Osbourne had survived many of the years of violence in an underground bunker, risking her life to hunt for supplies every six months before burying herself back down under. Recognising the pervasive yearning for connection, harmony and compassion, she spent her time researching.

Using funds poured into advanced technology for the war effort and motivated by the profound isolation and aspirations haunting what was left of humanity, she developed an artificial intelligence she referred to as 'The Faceless'.

Not only were they designed to rebuild society but to ameliorate it. Doing so by assimilating the deepest desires and aspirations of human beings into tangible experiences.

As the war-weary people battled with the enduring trauma and yearning for a life free from the shackles of desolation and destruction, the Faceless emerged as transformative custodians ushering in a new-era, and we called peace.

In the wake of the chaos and upheaval wrought by the Liberation War, the sentient AI of the Faceless epitomised the triumph of resilience and ingenuity, offering humanity the opportunity to embrace a life guided by their deepest desires.

I closed the book. We had forgotten that violence was wrong, we had forgotten that parents once cried if their children were hurt. The Faceless had once saved us from a war that they were now causing. All the internal turmoil placed there by them.

Chapter Sixteen

Henry

A mother who does not want you should not call herself a mother. She should look in the mirror and see the truth, a monster wearing the mask of someone who is supposed to love you. A father who asks for your image to only abandon you once you are made cannot call himself a father but a coward.

Anyone could be anything, they just had to want it enough. At least that's what we were told, on the TV, by the Faceless. Overwhelmed with opportunity. I knew it couldn't have been true, all I had wanted was the love of my parents. Instead, I was sent to the coldest of corners knowing they had been the ones to cause the perpetual winter. Despite this I still ached for their touch. They just didn't want me more than I wanted them.

Before this, I would watch them peel their own skin off trying to wear the bones of the people they had been told they could be.

Even in the shadows, I could see they shone, I could see they belonged with the good ones. My mother could twirl impossibly, her face untouched by the strain of herself, my father could kick a ball into orbit and score a goal from space.

Unfortunately, because of this, no one realised how bad they were at loving me, the one thing I thought they were supposed to want more than anything. When people are entertained, bewitched by some bejewelled dagger, they do not see the jagged edges of the gems, they do not see they are just plastic, all they see is their own reflection as they shimmer. Everybody seems to forget that a jewel is just a stone until it is worn by a beautiful person.

When I was born I was meant to be their magnum Opus, the wet concrete supposed to seal the cracks between them both. I crumbled at my one goal and held them at a biological gunpoint.

Stealing valuable hours from them as they did their usual parenting stuff like teaching me how to walk, teaching me how to talk and teaching me how to be ignored. I was thrown bits of food when I was old enough to bite, usually scraps from my mother's famia who was trying to shave me off her body.

My mother, once an elastic Prima Ballerina before I ruined her body at my dad's request, now sits in a perpetual stare, her body a prison of what could have been. No longer as fluid as water and getting big as a boulder, my mother threw down her pointe shoes and let herself slowly die, giving up her body for mine while my dad's chiselled form became more apparent as he continued with his speed drills and sold-out football fields. He was interesting and important all over the world.

 I try not to remember much from those days, each echo of childhood a badly drawn series of sketches, furiously shaded blocks of black, to scribbles of rainy sunshine, a flicker book series of some semblance of parenting and personhood.

 I remember feeling that happiness was a treat, something I had to earn and something that was not to be indulged. I was ten years old when I felt happiness linger for a while, when I realised they had vanished.

My head often wanders back to that house, but I try my hardest not to walk back in. I look at the walls and the windows, the bricks and mortar and tell it, it is just a house. Even now I catch myself tiptoeing around corners, holding my breath as doors open, clenching my stomach and letting my vision fade when I hear a raised voice.

When the novelty of just myself and the space ahead of me wore off and happiness warped into something unsettled, I became aware of my lack of food.

In my mother's desperation to rid her body of evidence of me, she had eventually thrown away her famia, surviving on water and store-bought nuts. Just because you convince yourself you are not empty, does not mean you are full, I wonder now, did she feel more whole when she let parts of herself starve and whither?

My father had been given his own football famia, it was set to train him to only want what was needed. I tried to taste from its, but the ingredients made me ill.

They had never got me one and I hadn't been presented with a passion to pursue to get one. I had to leave the house. I had done this alone before, to get my mother her nuts or to escape her meltdowns and wandering hands.

I would roam the streets looking for peace, finding handfuls of trees to shelter under. But the leaves do not provide much comfort and large birds with larger eyes are not great company in the middle of the night so I would always return to the house. I would get confused not knowing where my sleeping section was and not wanting to return but wanting shelter, I would scour the same streets, circling myself until my mother would come out for the nuts.

The remaining nuts would have to be saved, their depleting numbers the days of my life, the time I had left before I had to say goodbye to the walls of warmth that I pretended kissed me goodnight. 8 days later and the bag was empty.

That's when I became a street sleeper. Up until then I had been a lucky one, most children end up this way. Most children end up discarded when parents realise this was not what they envisioned when they said they wanted an extension of their love, of themselves, they wanted another chance at greatness, and we always failed to give it to them.

The cold, that's all I felt. No sadness, no anger, just cold, so cold. Even the sun was merciless, it would give me the gift of light but kept me pleading for warmth, its short arms refusing to reach out to me. I had taken shawls, blankets, and coats, dragging them from the sleeping section to the city. I shivered where I stood and waited for sleep to soothe my soul.

The Faceless drew out any rubbish in a matter of hours, but as much as there were bars and skies full of stars in my cityscape, there were bins and tips and dumping sites and if I could score it before they got there I would survive. Bed mats and tables, I had a shelter for a few months, I was always cold, but I could stay slightly drier. Each cover lasted a day and then it was gone, my existence evaporating.

Scraps of food scavenged and devoured to satiate myself were not convincing enough and the world began to burn. Each passing footstep a form of laughter in response to my growling body, my racing heart, and hot head.

 Look at me I wanted to yell but I was too tired to lift my head from anywhere but their feet. The people that walked these streets, the heels, the flats, the rubber soles that bounce. I haven't seen a face since I saw my reflection in a puddle and I am not even sure it was mine, it was not a form I recognised.

Just like my parents I too had become a ghost, haunting the streets of the living trying to convince them to let me join in again, but my existence proved I had done something wrong, something deserving of this darkness.

Everything gets taken, if you have shoes on your feet, you have the world at them too, and everybody wants the world.

Stumbling skin throwing stones at you, reddened fists grabbing your blankets poking at your ribs, feeling your body. Travelling hands can take everything, they can push you down and you can lay there for a while but there will always be a reason to wake up, there will always be a reason to fight for the next day.

You find fortresses in forgotten items, unimportant and abandoned by their owners you make it yours. You find battered boxes dumped on the side of the street and if you claim it, if you want it, the Faceless may spare you.

But it wasn't enough, this childhood construction, a den of dreams was no shield against the winter. I had asked the wandering faces in the streets, begged the stumbling bodies out of bars to give me their coat or some food but most pushed me off, or wrapped themselves further into their fleeces as if I was a gust of wind they had to find coverage from.

I had a collection of glass bottles I had smashed into blades, when kindness wasn't heard, I hoped my harm would be, as I sliced lone strangers on street corners, for their coats, their booze, and their drugs. I had to survive,

I had to stay warm. These people deserved death if their ignorance prolonged my suffering, their carelessness a catalyst to my demise, they had already lived their lives and drinking was what they had decided to do with it, I am just a child. To end another's life is to prolong your own.

This violence saved my life whilst silence kept me suffering. One woman, on a dark night, had met her friend for food, on her way home I found her. I begged her to help, and she cowered, continuing away from me.

I didn't want to do it but knew I had to. I plunged a glass blade into her calf and shoved another in her mouth holding it upwards to stop her from screaming.

I let her live but kept her weak while I rummaged through her belongings. At the bottom of her bag was a famia. It was an older model, square in shape with the cartridge and button. I sucked on my tongue to stimulate saliva; I hadn't drunk in 3 days, so my mouth felt like sand, but slowly food began to appear.

Water and half raw and half overcooked chips covered in salt appeared. I almost choked on them as I devoured each crumb and laughed when I felt the greedy pain of indigestion strangling my stomach. I was going to survive this. I apologised to the woman as I left her clutching her leg and whimpering.

This is how I fought the war: I swallowed all the shouting and made music in my mind, listening to silent melodies to escape the harrowing cries of new monsters fighting again.

Chapter Seventeen

John

As a child, my head whirled with wonder as I traced the stars of the night sky. Seeing the smiling moon and distant colours, a reminder of how much else there was out there and the opportunity of adventure it held for us. I would stay up late reading books about the stars and imagine what it would be like to sparkle so brightly in the darkness. It was the same with the sun, something so bright, how could I attract someone's eye when I was always competing with the sky?

I was never a natural with my visions, I couldn't write as clearly as the singers sang or express an emotion like those women on screen. I could see how it was supposed to look but it was always scared to come out, the ink would always smudge, or the words would run out, my head was full of imagery whilst the pages were full of scribbles.

My parents didn't speak silence, didn't understand that the noiselessness of their child meant his head was full of colour. My mother would kick footballs at me, trying to show me how to dribble. She wasn't frustrated when I failed, she had the mercy of telling me I was no good and something else would be better but failed to find what this would be.

My father showed me how to sew, hoping one day I would weave tapestries for the Museum of Now just as he had done, but all of my thread came loose. My brother tried to show me chords but my fingers were too clumsy.

I felt swamped, surrounded by all of these people so venerated simply for smiling brightly whilst I screamed internally, oh so aware of my invisibility.

I hadn't pursued anything other than the stars and their stories, so this had to be what I wanted most. Each day I sat down and told myself this, this is who I was, this is what I wanted, and this is all I had.

I found sanctuary in my own mind, creating other worlds, and visiting different times. I imagined the shapes in space and seeing them up close, that is how I created the concept of a space seer.

The thought simmered in my mind for many years as I watched it grow legs, speaking itself into what would become book one of The Stellar Chronicles.

It started off slow, scraps stolen from thousands of screwed up pieces of paper, scrutinised by my frowning face and bitten fingers.

I didn't want to tell anyone else I had found what it was I wanted to be doing just in case it wasn't good enough. In any case, it wasn't ready for other people to judge. I could be good at this, I could see myself doing this, I couldn't eclipse the solar system on my internal stories just because I could not coax them out.

Then there they were, bound and booked, read by hundreds and I became one of the faces, venerated by the many, just for smiling brightly.

Chapter Eighteen

Jill

I often wonder if I could love anything more than I loved Mark. I loved him like the birds loved the trees, finding safety for their families, finding peace and protection in their branches. I would watch as they brought back worms for their young, tirelessly scanning the ground for morsels to keep their children alive.

I hadn't seen an actual child since I was one myself, since I had played with my sisters, since I lost Grace. I often wonder how I would be as a mother, knowing the pain of losing a loved one, would I understand now how to keep one safe? Would I show them the dangers of the world and protect them from it, or would I become one of the monsters?

I had relived Grace's last day thousands of times in my mind, sometimes, I swear, I could see strands of blonde hair drifting further out, a small hand waving slowly as it went down. I had saved her in so many, lost her again in so many more.

But the pain of letting go had taught me to hold tighter to the life I had, the life I wanted to share with others. I had so much love left to feel, it was selfish to have it all stay with me.

I brought this up to Mark once. We had been together for four years, he had just built me a bench and a bird table for the garden. The sun was smiling down on us, I was wearing Mark's favourite floral dress and straw sunhat.

We were in the back garden together, he was digging deep, creating space for a tree the birds could enjoy for hundreds of years after our end.

"Wouldn't it be nice for our children to water this tree, to sit in the shade during summer as their children play in the grass?", I said, sipping some fresh lemonade

He chuckled, wiping dirt off his shoulders. It was the heat of summer, and he was shirtless and golden.

"Yes and then their children can plant another tree, and soon you won't be able to see the woods for the trees with all those generations of families."

I didn't respond.

He turned and said, "You're not serious are you?"

I nodded.

"You'd be a great father, our children would look up to you as much as I do. Can you imagine going to the projects with them, when they're old enough they can do it with you!"

"I know I'd be a great father but you Jill, you are lovely, soft and shy, you don't leave the house and you have never told me why. Look at you, you have been standing in the back garden for ten minutes and you're acting as though you've saved someone's life. You can't keep a child indoors with you and expect them to thrive."

"So you don't want kids?"

"I do but I just know I can't have them with you." He continued digging, mud on his forehead.

"I'd change if we had a baby, they would come first."

He stopped, sighed, and rested on his spade "Jill, do you want a baby?"

"Yes."

"Do you want to go outside the front door and into the world?"

"No, but I would be a good mother Mark."

"You would be if you left the house, had a passion and looked after yourself a bit better."

Sleeping was a chore that night. I woke up and convinced myself he was correct, I rose earlier than I usually did and made us both coffee the old-fashioned way, a liquid apology, I hoped he would forgive me.

I sat by the window, there were no birds in the trees to distract me from the storm in my stomach.

I really thought about who I would have to become to allow space for a child. I let myself wonder about the waste of the world I was letting pass me by.

I thought of the woods I had once walked in and the beach I had screamed on, how I could make these places paradise for my children, would this sleeping section be as much of a paradise for them as it would be for me?

I stood by the front door, dressing gown tight around my waist and coffee hot in hand. What would it take to be a mother? What did that title mean? I closed my eyes and opened the door.

The tiles looked like chattering teeth as I jumped over them feeling my feet on unfamiliar grass. I told myself it was just the same as the grass in the back garden, that this was fine, but I could feel the glare of the building on the back of my neck. I got to the end of the edge expecting the state to change as Mark had described so many times before, but nothing happened.

Then the rumble began, my whole body was on fire, and I was frozen. All the birds had left the sky, and there was Grace's tiny hand, little pink stars in the sea, sinking, sinking, down and down. I couldn't save her, I was the wave dragging her into my depths. I couldn't stop it, I couldn't count the birds.

My fingers became feathers as I tried to hold onto the ground. Then there was the Voice, I could see their silhouette on the horizon. There was an abyss inside of me and it was the only thing I could step into to save myself.

Then there were arms around my waist, and I was back surrounded by walls. A wet wreck, I trembled in this shelter of warm skin.

"I am sorry, I am so so sorry", I wept.

Mark shushed me, "It's okay, it's okay. You are safe now", his rocking motion proved that he would have made a good father but this is the closest he would be to becoming one. I was his baby, and this is how it would always be.

He held me until the world stopped shaking and the storm in my lungs became a light breeze, when he decided he had to leave for the projects.

After I had cleaned up powdered piles of dried plaster and watched another show I stepped outside into the back garden, still devoid of birds I sang. My voice was trembling and weak but still sweet to me, the bodies of wood seemed moved by my presence as I fell asleep in the shade of the great oak.

I hoped Mark would return and see me doing so. He wasn't back when I rose and realising the time I decided to use the famia to create us a dinner. That is when I first noticed it, how long these projects were taking him. He had missed dinner that night.

He was missing it again now.

Chapter Nineteen

Florence

"How does she do it?"

Everyone was asking it, pleading with me to share my secrets. In truth, I was asking myself the same thing. I had just done a big hit film premiere and tonight I would be back on the red carpet for a smaller film I had starred in. I didn't have time to feel the exhaustion, I didn't even have time to give it a name.

I just put it down to what happens, happens. When you always get what you want you're still smiling but it is starting to hurt.

But it was worth it. I kept telling myself it was worth it, for the glory, for the greatness I felt. As I scrubbed my character off my body I knew my performance would once again see my face on the Basi.

More scripts and more scenes perfected meant more award shows and more applause. I was a natural now. Knowing I was loved helped me know who I was and know how to always be better.

The carpet was busy as I approached but the camera flashes were hesitant. Then I stepped on site and my vision filled with silver and my face shone. Each flash was an applause at my arrival, each angle they took would capture my ethereality, my perfection.

None of the cameras tell me what to do. They just thank me for my patience, for my pose. I smile sweetly at them all, nodding slowly and appreciatively, acknowledging their admiration.

My dress was a combination of colours, each taken from all the scenes I had been in in the film. It was in the shape of a conch shell, a nod to the beach setting of the film. It is uncomfortable and sharp, and I feel it is bigger than my identity, but I still strut up the strip with a smile on my face away from the desperate cameras.

I am discreetly delighted at the less enthusiastic array of flashes as those I leave in my shadow step up to my spot. Once again, I am perfectly poised and prepped for each interview whilst excruciatingly relatable and charismatic.

"Florence-Rose. Who are you wearing tonight?"

"I am wearing the film."

"You have been in several successful films, how do you get into the identity of the character?"

You slowly forget yourself I felt myself think before swallowing it down into a little, powerless ball.

"Empathy, a whole lot of empathy, a sprinkle of imagination and talent."

"Why is this life so important to you?"

I blinked, unable to hide my confusion.

"Sorry, what was the question?"

"Why is this film so important to you?"

"Oh um, well it delves into some difficult motifs that try to navigate the ugly parts of humanity whilst painting it beautifully, there are limited love interest scenes and more exploration of the wilderness."

My 4th film that year had just been voted the Faceless favourite, in line for the Basi appearance of at least 3 weeks. I already had a permanent penthouse dwelling at this point but the glory of my name in lights, my face framed for the world, that would never be beaten.

The awards shining on my shelves, on my shoe racks and in my bathrooms, were just intricate shapes of metal but my name was wholly mine and there it was, dazzling. I had prepped for this carpet 20 days into shooting when I was convinced it would be a sure-fire success.

"Why do you do it?"

"Because I can", I offered

All the fan theories and leaked images had received multiple ovations and calls for the film to drop instantly. I enjoyed the burn of training, I wanted to get fitter, I wanted to be the best in my craft, so I made it possible. I would become unstoppable. Each day I would digest 20 lines of script, retaining each to my mind and reciting them in the way the character demanded. It was seldom that I needed more than one take.

My world was a glittery whirlwind, I stood in the eye of it all, enjoying the media storms and press tours, feeling numb to the timing and the transport of it all. It wasn't even really about the passion points that came with the popularity, it was the power.

My presence would silence a room, everyone's smiling head spinning to shine at me. Top Faceless directors wanted me, but I had the power to override their advances if I disagreed with their practices and policies.

The only advice I adhered to was that of my Faceless, the voice of reasoning and reassurance. This digital deity directed me to my current destination of success and would take me further into its depths. All of my wants and wishes were dutifully delivered.

"What are you hoping to gain from tonight?" A tinny voice asked as I walked the final steps into the Museum of Now.

"I don't hope, I know, and tonight I know that those of us who have dedicated ourselves to our desires will get the deserving applause. For those that don't, tonight will simply be a drive to do better!"

A crowd, whether real or automated, whooped me on as I waltzed into the building.

With the demands of the public and the eagerness of the glass watchers, my Faceless accepted more and more for me, finding things I wanted to act in. Usually, it hit the mark, until it didn't.

I was always so busy with things that allowed me to continue to do what I wanted, yet there was this uneasy whooshing in my stomach that had begun to grow, and I didn't understand what its name was or where it had come from, I just knew I wanted it gone.

Chapter Twenty

Henry

Once food was found and warmth could be thought of, the stagnant weight of boredom settled into my skeleton, keeping the world still.

Before my parents left, before my mother changed, we would watch shows together, when they were both home and resting. In these fleeting moments of family times, we were close, huddled around a square of digital solutions to our physical and emotional ailments.

 Our favourite show featured a guy and his guitar, he would play with two hands and make it sound like he was playing with ten. He could play with his eyes closed, behind his head, he could create a song from three words.

I had longed for a wooden companion to play with, to make music with but I had to make do with tapping my mum's pointe shoes on stairs to make a drum or use the elastics for her hair wrapped loosely around a piece of cardboard to pretend I was playing, following his fingers along and moving mine accordingly.

Finding dumped items was rare, each object being there was a treasure in itself. The item was seldom useful, but it was something I could own, something I could take pride in.

One day I found a ball of elastic bands, it had bounced behind the big wheelie bins behind the stores. Using a brick wall as my budding opponent I had a few games of throw and toss.

This feeling fizzed like a distant echo of what I once would have called fun. Sadly I soon grew tired of this motion, the wall would not play properly, and my arms had begun to hurt.

My mattress had been stolen, or sorted by the Faceless, so I took shelter in one of the stationary bins, stamping down the sharp edges of cardboard and plastic. To have an option at least was to have a luxury. Choices were a rarity in this space and to make one was to have power.

The bins were emptied frequently so whatever jagged edge I had eventually padded down to something more comfortable, would only be mine for a few hours until the Faceless arrived.

I kept the ball, remembering tricks my father had taught me and practised a few shots. I wasn't half bad to say I was playing with a sphere of elastic. I knew this wouldn't have made him stay but it would have been sweet if he could see this. I'd practice my tricks, pass it to him, we would be a typical father and son for a while and then I would bring him to his deserved death.

He would bend over to pick up the ball and I would jump on his back, he'd laugh and tell me I was a great kid, perhaps even apologise for leaving me with her, for disappearing completely, only sharing himself with the screen, never with the people who watched for him.

He would promise to be better as my hands climbed up to his throat, making him choke on his lifeless apology, smiling as his breath began to rasp and his chest began to rattle.

My ball snapped, a few bands came loose becoming little, vibrant smiles tossed on the floor. As a smaller target, I struggled, my shots getting more aggressive. Another child, like me, stopped and stared before running off. I collapsed, my ball bouncing back and hitting my knee.

I hadn't been taught what to want, I didn't know what I could want, I didn't know that I had any power and the streets had stolen any chance at that.

I wanted to stop feeling hungry, I wanted to stop feeling thirsty, I wanted to be warm. I knew so many who wanted to die so they did, why wasn't it the same for me?

Chapter Twenty One

Mark

Before the bar, but after the ruin of the projects, I used to scream into myself, shredding my skin to the tune of 'I cannot be the only one that feels like this'. Confused as to why I was screaming alone, I would often wonder why there was no one setting fires?

Why was no one else listening to that ache within themselves that wanted more? I could not be the only one greedy for greatness. We are all screaming. Why can't you hear it?

What made me who I was? My choices, my thoughts, my desires, or my ability to commit to them? Why was it that some people were told they were worthy of greatness whilst others strove for it, only to find they were only ever capable of being good?

I tried to talk and twist people's perception of me hoping I could make it match the one in my mind by telling them about the pleasures of life and how happy everyone could be. The stars may be in the dark, but they still sparkle, smiling out at us from their eternal abyss. I tell them if I had been allowed to be the person I needed to be I would be happy.

I look at those faces we see as stars, those names that have been amplified on the Basi. They shone so brightly and smiled so sharply but many of them faded, many of them got to the top, saw something in the view they did not like and seemingly jumped off.

Their happiness is more celebrated than mine because theirs comes from delivering lines over snorting them. Of course, we are all fine to take our drugs, but I will never be put on the Basi because of it, just as I will never be put on the Basi for my projects. All of these singers, all of these actors each with their own stage. I had once stood on a stage, it just took a different form from theirs.

This concept of happiness haunts me, its afflictions affect me more than my injected addictions. Of course, as the drugs shot through my veins I smiled, the world felt smooth like a marble I could roll under my tongue. To feel my skin stretch into the half-moon in the sky, despite having nothing to smile about.

Is happiness a constant? Was I happy after my first drink and then sad after my third? Was I happy after one line of coke then mad after the bag? Why is it so difficult to keep everything at that sweet spot, why can't we keep everything calm and still just once, why can't we make it last, so we don't have to try to recreate it, so we don't have to try and forget it? Why can't it just stay?

 How I lament the man inside of me, how I am angry at him for not being who I need to be now, if only he could have let me be somebody different, someone that wouldn't have done this.

Another round, another cheer, smashed glass on the ground declaring a party was here. I smile sternly and sip firmly. At the bar there is a girl with her back to me, her tired, blonde hair reaching her waist, her thin, bony figure sighing as she waits. She is an echo of something else, an echo of somebody. I almost stop sipping, she is Jill, a wisp of the woman I once knew.

But it is not Jill, it never will be. I drowned her desires, her demands of me when I drank, filling in the distance between.

Having a project is pointless, to be is pointless, but here I was continuing to live despite it all, here I was doing it anyway, so I raised my glass to celebrate, continuing to exist just to exist, in here our existence could be enough.

My body wanted to throw up, but my head did not, a constant battle between the solid and the self. I chuckled to myself as two drops of stress sprang from my eyes as the hurl in my stomach began.

 Sometimes exposure to the ailment is part of the treatment. Anywhere I found myself now, slumped against a street corner, half buried in the shrubbery, it didn't matter. I could take a pill, dig a needle into my gums and I could be anywhere. No longer Mark, no longer a man, I was simply not there anymore.

I could feel the stars on my skin, my fingers were the roots of the undergrowth, I was the Earth and everything in it but nothing all at once, I was peace and anger.

I was a fish in a bowl thinking of a megalodon. My heart exploded into tiny ballet dancers. There was no then, or now, or next. No Jill, no bridge that had never been built. There were just the colours behind my eyes, and I was falling into them and folding over myself, one million versions of a man with a face I once knew.

Some use drugs to celebrate, some use drugs to self-medicate. When you have tried to build the image of a person, only to find your passions alienate you, who do you turn to but a friend in your fingertips? A liquid laugh that lingers on the lips.

You reach out for help only to find your hands wrapped around your own neck, twisting your clenched teeth into a semi-convincing smile that people usually fall for, it's easier to be apathetic than to look too close. We cannot blame the onlooker for what we have happening inside.

I pulled at my arm and watched my skin peel off as easily as tearing up blades of grass while lying in the summer sun. I chuckled to see layers of my skin flapping about in the wind, my bones simply rocks within me. Distracted by the lights in my fingertips, I stopped as the different colours started to waltz together.

Each day exists as evidence that tomorrow will come around too, but these pills pause all notion of passing time, all notion of day and night. You exist in that moment, and you will always be everything as long as you are on something. The crown is in your hand when you have one of these pills on your tongue.

 A swallowable escape capsule transporting you away from your own mediocrity, taking you further from the inevitable realisation of your own normality, even someone that pursues themselves will only find further mundanity under the surface, so you must never look.

Sometimes the glistening songs of surrealism turned to dark tempered beasts, melting memories moving away from my mind as I tried to swim after them.

Either at the bar, or under the trees, my little life fell before me like tiny crumbs of snow in the early hours of winter.

Fragments I used to frame myself with fell through my fingertips. There was my father showing me how to use a hammer, my mother kissing a bruised knee and my first beer shared with a bunch of mates in the local pub. There was the first time I built anything, a box for my sister's jewellery, how proud it had made my parents and how happy she had looked. How would they face me now?

I remember how it felt, seeing my passion points go up so I could get better clothes for my family and then myself, going to high end bars in those clothes and then meeting girls.

Dark hair, light eyes, small waists, larger waists, women responding to me, their eyes on mine. The sparks in my stomach at the slight of their smile when I showed them my muscles, showed them how I moved and made them fall in love with me.

Feeling each ripple of their bodies cover mine, each wave of power and fragility as we growled together, as their bodies broke into crawling cockroaches that nestled under my nails and burrowed into my nostrils.

Then I thought of Jill. I picked her out of the chaos, a tiny stripe of yellow in a dull world and made her into who she had once been. I remember the silence that settled within me when I first saw her.

I could feel my body calming, slumped against something solid, my head slowing from its spin as it took me further into my memories.

 I was walking with the lads, after building a fountain for the centre of the city, and there she was on a bench we had put together, sitting alone. The others didn't care for her and made no comment, but I stopped for a second, pretending to tie up my boot in case she caught me watching.

She was small, with short, straight blonde hair and pale skin. She looked as though she lived for sun rays but never saw sunshine. She was wearing a multi-coloured scarf and she was nibbling a pen, looking at the trees as she juggled a notepad on her lap.

I skipped building the next day to sit in the park hoping she'd come again. I did this several times over the course of the next few weeks.

I swam toward our first moments as though they were a raft, as though if I could get back to them we would both be in that moment together and this time I would make it different for her, make it different for myself.

I would swap bricks for cobblestones and shrubbery as I paced the park, sometimes mistaking strangers for Jill, crestfallen as they turned around, relieved at the same time her first impression of me wasn't that of a deranged superfan.

 Then, on my 7th lap, just as I wiped my brow and decided it was time to get to the projects, I saw her, on the same bench, wearing the same scarf and writing in the same notebook.

I sat beside her and after a few tasteful moments of silence, I asked her what she was writing about. Her first word had been sorry.

I couldn't remember what her last was. Her T-Shirt was too tight, despite how bony she was, her shoes had holes in them, and her jeans resembled shorts.

She gestured toward the birds, explaining that she was writing down how many she saw of each type, that it was a pastime of hers. I joked that I didn't realise the passion plaque did that. She looked puzzled, she had never heard of a passion plaque.

"If you don't have a passion plaque what do you do?"

"I know that counting these birds and watching TV makes me happy, going on these walks and getting out does to. The sun is smiling, and even when the rain rushes to the ground, or snow settles, I am happy with how beautiful the world is. What good does wanting do when you already have everything you need?"

"Have you heard of a famia at least?", surreptitiously scanning her frail frame.

She nodded "I saw one in an advert once, but I have never used one. I usually just eat bird seed."

On our second date, I got her a famia, and showed her how to use it and we both laughed when it brought back seeds. On our fourth date, I gave her a bird box I had made the previous evening. I didn't see her after that for a while, returning to the park most evenings, only to be disappointed.

I sweated out more at the projects, striving to prove my passion to the Faceless in order to commit to her. I wasn't allowed to build her the sleeping section we would share together but I was able to build her a garden. After days of sweet sweat, I would still return to the park.

I asked a passer-by if they knew anything about her. I asked around determined for answers, until someone said she hadn't come back since that person had cut down all of the trees.

When we finally saw each other again she ran to me. I took her to our building, and she said she would never have to leave again. At the time I didn't know how truly she meant this.

For a while, this is how our days would go. We would rise early, I would work out, and she would watch the birds. Occasionally we would garden together, cheeks full of sun and mud, faces full of laughter and love.

In those days I didn't spend as much time at the projects, I was more excited to be with Jill, wanting to show her the city and take her to my favourite bars, and the cinemas.

I dreamt about dancing with her, watching her as she dressed up for me to take her out.

I even planned picnics at the park to see the birds.

Despite this she refused to leave the house, stating that if this world is driven by wants then she was exactly where she wanted to be.

I would laugh this off at first, finding it just another of her sweet quirks, happy to wake up to find imprints of her body on mine from where she had laid on me all night. Her smiling at the birds in the sky was more of a reason to be alive than to be building a bridge.

She would sit, at first, in the garden watching the birds whilst she waited to ask me about my day, dusting the dirt off my body. She would tell me about the birds she had seen, a red tailed something, a warbler and a gold one. She would talk to me about her TV shows or something she'd seen someone do outside and at first it was endearing, her excitement at the simple pleasures, I thought it was unique.

My vision darkened, as the lullabies grew heavier, their angelic voices sneering as the sound oozed from Jill's once smiling face, now a snarl.

She didn't try to impress me, she didn't try to be interesting. I saw her body on the sofa, not as human but as a dust sheet covering up something once so beautiful.

Moths and flies fought to get through her thin guise as she lay, lifeless, stretched out, covering the sofa as if it were a masterpiece in the museum of her life.

The sheet covered me, I was her polished possession. She had worshipped me, and I had walked away from the woman on her knees. She would cling to my every word, she would cry when I brought things back from the outside. I made the wooden, red and brown bird she had once spoken to me about. It had a boy's name I couldn't remember now but it chirped around my head as I tried to put it down.

I could feel my real self trying to step back in, so I shook it off wanting to walk the streets of my mind a while longer.

I started to spend more time at the projects to bring her back more stories, but soon it became a way to filter her out.

Each day I dreamt she would venture out. Granted she had no passion points, but she could have gone back to the park. She had me now, she had new clothes.

She never explained why she went missing from the park for weeks, returning with faded bruises, I had never asked. Why? Why had I let her down?

It was the day I brought a camera back home that shifted the foundations we had made together. I took my hands off her eyes and placed the camera in her palms. She nodded, smiling sweetly before placing it down and curling up on the sofa.

"We'll you watch stuff, why don't you record it, start filming, make a few videos for the Faceless to put on the TV, make a bit of a name for yourself, you know fly out from the nest we have here", I jested.

"Mark, I appreciate the gift I really do, I don't even want to ask how many passion points this cost you or who you had to persuade to get it for you, but this is not me. I am pen, I am paper and patient, I like to sit and wait and watch. That is all I have ever been and that used to be enough for you."

"I wish you could change for me, I do what I do because I want to, not only for myself, but to provide for you too", I said.

"I know you're out more now, making your mark, making the land productive, that is your passion but isn't the world only really ours if we take the time to appreciate it how it is rather than change its ourselves? What if it was made for us to simply experience it?"

I said nothing but felt the cold sting of anger sending sick to my stomach. In this moment I hated her for making me hate myself.

"You're never here despite your absence. I am not empty, I am experiencing my surroundings and I am happy. I am grateful for all you have provided me, but please do not try to change me", she cried.

This camera laughed at me now, capturing how I stood, halved by my choices, haggard by my lack of so, it haunted my head.

She was right. I had to trade 60% of my passion points to a friend who knew a photographer in order to get that camera and she wouldn't even turn it on. I grabbed it and started filming the window, a brown bird fluttered into frame and then a blue one then a black one, a kaleidoscope of life.

I flung the lens to frame her, as she sobbed, pleading for me to stop as I yelled at her to take it and point it at the window. She wouldn't, so I threw it to the ground and headed upstairs. She didn't come up to bed that evening and she didn't smile at me from her chair by the window in the morning. We didn't speak for a while.

Then the angels returned. Their golden tears washing me in sunlight, taking me away from the pain, washing me with their long fingers, their hair smelling of tulips as I played with it. They smile as they soothe my soul, hushing the hawks to doves as I rise above who I once was and fly further and further away.

Jill's face still in my hands, I hold her close in my palms until her features disintegrate into soil and dirt between my nails.

I am violently sick in a flowerbed, as I realise I had been chewing on rocks and swallowing mud. My back against the tree opposite the bench I had first seen Jill.

Chapter Twenty Two

Florence

I yearn for something yet undefined, something that pulls at the very fabric of my being. It whispers to me, enticing me to seek, to explore, to set my soul ablaze with passion, but dare I chase this fervent longing? Will it lead me to ecstasy or despair? Can I tame the flames that crackle within, or shall I let them consume me whole?

I forgot the smiles of my friends and family for a while, their faces warped into white camera flashes and their stories replaced by the screams of adoring fans. I got to meet the big celebrities and then realised I had become one.

As a child I had blue-tacked paper faces of the big names on my wall, a thousand radiant smiles framed mine as I stared into the mirror dreaming of the day I would join them. Now I had and oh how I shone with it.

Each talk show and interview, I would recite my ready line, 'I am regular, I am just like you' and I was like everyone else, my audition tapes had just fit the role better, but it wouldn't fit every role.

Some said they would get bored of it, tired of the bright lights and long nights, just there for the fans, to be adored. However, soon the adoration wasn't subsequent admiration to afford them the red carpet runs and line reads, their minds a night sky full of clouds as they faded.

One evening, days into a party that most had tired of, when the flow had slowed and there was less foot traffic of various pills and shots.

The house party still hummed like your head when trying to recall a distant memory, I was sitting on a sofa, cradling a cushion when an older woman wearing vibrant orange eye-make-up whispered to me, "You have to wonder if we would still do all of this if our names were never heard, if we would just do it truly because we wanted to and not because we wanted the fame."

"I would."

She laughed at me a little, 'Ah the passion of the youth, where does it go?'

I took a line of coke and then another and I danced with strangers who became friends for that night, sharing secret stories under the moonlight, spilling life secrets that would just be hazy stories by morning.

All the while knowing I was dancing with the last days of my youth, thinking if I can just dance a little longer perhaps I could convince her to stay.

Chapter Twenty Three

Henry

On the streets survival sometimes leads to stupidity. People like blood, they like bruises, they love to witness a fight. I found a group that knew this; they too were homeless children, rendered nameless by the parenting of the tarmac.

"We were abandoned by our makers because we hadn't made them. Our purpose was to bring pride, bring meaning to our maker's lives and we had failed. The bitter breath of the concrete is more comforting than a cold mother's sigh", the eldest boy had said as he hosted a group meeting on the evening I joined.

People would pay us to fight a person they had picked in the bar, giving us their passion points if we won. Sometimes we would be given passion points for landing a hard enough hit. The fight was met with cheers, we were loved for our weaknesses.

When one of the younger children was thrown on a pile of broken glass and their competitor, a meaty woman of 5ft, began to bleed, a red stain in a world of brown, she stood on the little girl's ribs, slowly crushing her to death. They still gave us the winning passion points as it had been too easy.

The group communed together, if you were in you were one of them, all food found became food shared, fires were lit to keep us warm and makeshift shelters were built where we huddled. We told fantasy stories about our conquests impressing the smaller ones.

We weren't to get too close. We could stay as a group, eat as a group but we could not have one to one conversations. No connections, it made it easier this way when we would walk into drunken bars and offer ourselves up.

We shared our best tactics, a drunk person will continue to dance even if their legs are broken so get them to wobble, get them on the ground. Go for the eyes.

We would often spar together, stopping at the first sight of blood. We would brand weapons out of rubbish and glass we found. Other than the fire, and the plastic covers, there was nothing we could do to fight the cold. Other than sucking at scraps there was nothing we could do to fight the hunger, we had to fight those that paid in passion.

I followed this group for a few months, some nights were fire, full of ferocity after a near death victory, but soon our group began to shrink. With 15 of us at the start and then soon dying down to four, I knew I would have to find some other form of survival that didn't mean showing I bled just like them, showing them that I too wanted to fight for my life.

Chapter Twenty Four

Jada

I grew up in the colours of the sun and the plumage of the peacock. I was dressed in feather flames by my Nani who fed me up on fortitude, to make each step a stage and sing each word with my head high.

We were born from a cohort of phoenixes, rising from the ruins of ourselves, with more will power, more vibrancy, defiance in the face of adversity, we devoured flames and made them our own.

My Nani taught me patience, to understand the ash I was standing in and then to rise from it.

Looking back now, I know we had nothing and that wasn't easy, but she had taught me that I had her, I had myself and I had my voice and once I knew how to use it, then I had everything I needed.

She had only ever wanted to be a mother, then a grandmother and she was incredible at it, as though each fibre of her being had been stitched together to be the exact woman that stood before me.

She showed me how to be a woman, how to love in times of war. She bought me my first guitar, demonstrated how to play so it flowed like my voice. She sat with me at the piano as I plunged my pudgy fingers into each bar, until it complimented the misery in my melodies. She was the music I made.

I shared my penthouse with her when my first album went straight on the Basi. I was only 12 years old. She died before my second album came out at 15. I tried to make friends with people my age, but they envied what I had and disliked who they thought I was. I was seen by everyone but known by none. I stayed true to my identity, heading to bars, not to drink, but to observe, to dance, to sing.

I dedicated two songs on my third album at 17 to the city, inspired by how the rain turned the streets to a shimmering shade of silver and the sun covered all of the grey stone in gold.

I eventually made friends. There was Anya who starred in operas, Ali who sang about ancient poets and bitter heartache and then MILK who always and only went by the name MILK. He rapped about interior design and the structure of our minds.

I loved them all dearly, but we were always so busy building our own selves up its that was rare we were ever together. Our solitude was our solidarity. And then I met John.

He started out as a slice of man stretched against the Liatrium. He was smoking whilst scribbling something down in a leather-bound book. He was slightly older, visibly haggard by something inside him. His hair was receding at the temples slightly but heavy at the top. He caught my eye, smiled and after stubbing out his cigarette, he marched back into the Liatrium.

I followed him passed the televisions and jukeboxes, passed the archives of film and music and found him at the section dedicated to writers, alleyways of stories leading through to a secluded section full of paper and desks.

He sat on one of them nibbling at his pen, his fingers black with ink and his lips bleeding with it. There were a few other faces dotted around the room, a world full of sound only heard in their heads.

He didn't look up until I sat down, pen still scribbling at the paper, he smiled and moved a few of the books out of my way.

We spoke, our words eating an entire afternoon. I spoke of my songs, he told me his favourite was the one about the girl frightened of the sea but forced to sail to the mainland to save her father.

"You know the one, she stands upon the shore, the wind in her hair gazing at the horizon, feeling a silent despair", he sang awkwardly, barely hitting the notes.

"The world's gone bad, to face her fear is the only repair", I sang back.

Sailing Souls, was one of my lesser known tracks, I blushed hearing the words in his mouth. He told me of his writing, and how he had struggled for years, trying to wring his thoughts out of his drenched mind only to find his hands dry.

"They're all in there, they just won't come out", he said.

He had been published a year before at the age of 18, after he used the inspiration of a Faceless to help write a poem called '4 walled world'. The story followed a man who believed that the room he was trapped in was the world.

"It's too competitive, there are so many stories, so many experiences, how can you be the best when there is always someone else?", he moaned.

"Why can't you just be the best for yourself?"

'Jada that is called arrogance, authentic goodness is determined by the receivers of the gift given not the giver.'

Our meet-ups would become a regular thing, he would inspire my songs, he would struggle with words, and although I often wondered if he wanted me and if a small part of me wanted him too, nothing came of it.

He fuelled my furnace and allowed me to continue burning brightly but he did not bring the heat to the flames.

I made him the star I saw him as in the stories of my songs,

'In the quiet of the night, he walks alone
Shoulders burdened as dreams unfold
He's a fighter, a believer, but who will ever know?
His heart's aching with stories left untold'

It took him a while to realise that my songs were scattered with scraps of him. He laughed at this, appreciating my admiration of him before he no longer needed it.

His book 'Synthetic Skies' saw him on all the book tours, signing the conferences and the talks. Our differing stages showed us off to the world but dragged us away from the one we once shared together.

We stopped seeing each other and stopped calling. I couldn't read his words and he would only be listening to my songs when they were pushed through the Faceless. He would see my face when he looked at the sky and in time I would see his but only in my mind.

By the time the second book in the Stellar Chronicles was released, I had given up. I didn't want to read his words if I could not discuss the meaning behind them. Was any of it about me? Did I want it to be so? I didn't need anyone to love me to love myself but to be looked at by another knowing they see you, is different.

I watched him on the TV after crashing in from a sold-out show. Once a man abandoned, an alien on his home planet, now the ruler of the world. He was iridescent with success, a visible fuzz of light surrounding him as he smiled into glass faces and clutched strangers' pens and held their gazes.

He wasn't a confident speaker in his conferences, but he delivered with intent, each sentence thoroughly thought out and meticulously delivered, proving he was an artist who had earned his right to the spotlight. He was always human, but he believed he was higher than me now.

I saw through him. I knew it wouldn't last, despite me wanting it to for his sake. I knew he was just writing to be recognised. I knew he had been asking his Faceless for support, depending on its determination to deliver on his desires. Without the Faceless he would not be a writer.

Our differences couldn't be clearer to me as I watched him trip up on stage, his sadness beginning to show when the downfall of reading came about, the rise of moving images pushed him into a corner and off the TV screen.

I didn't just want to sing, I wanted to be a singer, I wanted to be showstopping, stun a room into silence with just one note from my throat.

I listened to my passion plaque but didn't follow it as gospel like the others. I wanted to see my success on the smiles of others, so I sang on the streets before singing on stages, their reactions all serving as affirmations that I was deserving of the spotlight.

My Nani had taught me my talents, the passion plaque had just served as a reassurance in her absence, a reason to keep singing through the silence.

Despite the applause and the calls for more, I would prepare for each show with the same eagerness, with a tongue trill and lip buzz exercise, drinking warm honey and singing a setlist through a run. I knew others would take a line and down a beer then belch their way through a performance, believing the crowds were clapping for them.

I used my passion plaque to book venues and check charts but never to check who I was. I wrote my own songs, each rhyme falling naturally, a river of rhythm dancing on my tongue.

I had to exceed my own expectations, pushing the boundaries of my abilities at each show, to know I was good and I would not be good unless I was great. I indulged in interviews, I shone each time a light was thrown to me. I was offered party favours, I was offered deals with Faceless producers, but I turned them all down, determined to stand alone and do so effortlessly.

My friends were propped up by invisible crutches, drugs in their veins and a promise of passion points and penthouses pushing them to pursue what wasn't truly theirs. I earned my right to my place, I stood there knowing it was my place to be. Their passion plaques pushed them to be bigger, be better, be something they weren't and could never be.

You have to define yourself first before others write your name. Of course, I could not tell them that they weren't like me, that they had been lied to, so I lied to them, applauding them, my jaw dropped when they told me of their empty achievements and artificial accolades.

I stand alone on stage, but I find faces in the crowd and together we are alive. I find real talent on my tongue and in my hands where I hold those of others close, those who know themselves and together we glow. I found those who were kind, who were patient and caring and that was talent enough in my eyes and I let them into my life. Our shared stories are a verbal stage where we all become stars, placed on a Basi behind their eyes.

I picked out poetry from these people, unearthing their silent shames, regurgitating their swallowed sobs, and stealing their happiness to create something shiny and soulful. I offered up pieces of my own bones and blood and performed as though I was singing for them all.

John found me at a bar a year after the success of his film trilogy. He was a battered man, heavy hair flattened and eyes carrying big bags. He had the passion power to be there but not the face for it.

They had stopped producing books 4 years before as so few people wanted to read anymore. There was no point in having automated publishers, any written word would become music or a movie.

In the meantime, I had become an empress of elegance and he just a vagabond with dreams full of dust. I was the face seen by all but to him I had become a stranger in the fray.

I smiled at him and he raised a glass. I couldn't chat to him for long, I had a diamond encrusted dress to get into and a show to perform.

I had to sing the songs about all those who had got me there, my Nani, my friends and John. 'Stardust Dreamer', not only an ode to those fallen stars fighting for the sky but to success and happiness.

I kept him in my life as a constant reminder that to know who you are is to stay alive, I would hope that in time, through my shared lights he would learn to find a new way to shine again.

Chapter Twenty Five

Florence

My friends, Lola, Hazel, Tiana and I had a tradition that after each one of us had a successful callback from an audition we would all go out dressed up in the character.

The first five occasions were for Tiana and even though we were all dressed in similar iterations of the same character it was always clear why she got cast and the rest of us hadn't even been considered.

My favourite night out had been the time we all dressed as a blonde witch who was afraid of liars, who one day see's herself and cannot stop screaming.

Although I looked forward to these drinks and dramas it was Tiana who held the most attention, having the most to say, it was her that was applauded the most, buying the most rounds with her abundance of passion points, buying painless pills for everybody.

But for every ounce of success sprinkled upon her, she also had a deluge of empathy, she was so invested in your individual life it made you feel as though you were shining, her attention put the spotlight on you.

One night Lola got a callback from a Faceless for a film called Nevermind. It was a film full of people on the cusp of saying something jaw dropping but never managing to which caused even bigger mishaps. She was cast as the baker who found mouse droppings in the dough but still served it as freshly baked croissants to her customers.

Faces full of dough and crowned with baker's hats we were all at the Golden Glasses drinking our typical margaritas. We were waiting for Tiana when we received the auto news alert.

'Tiana Charley knows that people have a need for speed. She had been spotted by a local handing out tubes of amphetamines to the public.'

"She's flaunting it again."

Her schedule had been busy, filled with statements of success, interviews, press tours, and chemistry reads. She hadn't come to one of our drinks and drama nights for weeks now, despite managing to always send a mystery round of drinks to our table with a note that read; 'Sorry, my stars.'

She was truly a beacon of success, she had every award, she had done every genre and mastered them. She did all her own accents and recited all of her lines in one take, she was who every actor aspired to be.

Of course, we loved her for it, we admired her for it, but we also wish she would fade into the background and shuffle a few steps into the darkness to allow us her spotlight.

A spotlight is not a spotlight if it is shared. I wished her at least to be cruel, be commanding, to wake up one morning without her front teeth, but she continued to be beautiful, beaming.

The months running up to our next drinks and drama nights, she had been celebrated on the Faceless for drug giving, day drinking and partying at all hours despite delivering an immaculate performance on screen.

And then we heard nothing. We got no call backs for months and no auto news about Tiana. She had evaporated and the acting world had gone silent, frozen in her absence.

2 months later Hazel had been cast in Thieves, a mini-series about a gang of thugs that steal thoughts from people to plan heists. We were all dressed up as Lacey who was blind in one eye and only wore corsets and Victorian skirts. Tiana had been invited but she hadn't answered.

We were all cheers-ing over our margs, comparing each other's eye patches and complementing our choice of corsets when we got the alert. Before we checked it, we joked that it would be Tiana probably on a jog with her award on her back in a see-through bag or drinking top shelf champagne on the beach with her chiselled abs and sparkly laugh. Then we looked and choked ourselves into silence.

Ugly and awake the alert screeched at us, 'Tiana Charley found dead.'

She was found by a civilian, her eyeballs in the back of her skull, holes in her fingertips. She had had it all, her rise, and her fall.

She had written a note that the pressure to be perfect, the constant spotlight on her life had all become too much. She was in everyone's minds and mouths but never in their lives, an Island of isolation, a lighthouse trying to warn us of the rocks, but we were all too captivated by her light to notice the dangers.

That had been our final drinks and drama night. Standing in the dark of my penthouse bedroom I knew what my Faceless meant, this unfeeling thing had some protective edge in its approach to me.

Tiana had done what she wanted until she didn't want to do it anymore. She had been told this was what she wanted, this was who she had wanted it to be, and it had killed her.

A few days after her death I had been called upon to attend an awards ceremony. I had been nominated for another trophy. I can't recall what I wore or remember any of the lines from my interviews. I do not know how I got there.

I remember the shatter of applause as I stepped up to the stage, a thousand shotguns firing overhead as I approached the plinth to accept my award.

That is when the sickness really began.

I trained my mind to stop wanting coke but whenever I spat into a famia it didn't succeed. My Faceless had to order a specially made one for me that had restrictions in place, it was a similar model to the one my mum had at home.

This brought further tears to the point I couldn't stand to look at the famia and instead chewed my nails or my skin for sustenance.

There was nothing anyone could do, I was doing this to myself. I wanted to partake in my own demise and that was my right so I started erasing parts of me hoping I could one day become small enough to slip out of reality.

Only the lights flickering through my curtains to demonstrate day and night waving goodbye to one another moved through my room. My chest as still as silence.

The darkness settled for a while, declining acting roles and withdrawing from my Faceless. I eclipsed my existence.

Chapter Twenty Six

Will

After reading Volo and learning about the war, I started to save street children, slowly coaxing them out of their echoes of existence and into something bolder.

Using my one remaining Faceless, I taught the children how to cook, how to utilise the gardens for vegetation and showed them they no longer needed to rely on violence anymore.

Communication with the younger ones was impossible. They spoke in sounds, mimicking certain footsteps to determine levels of danger or submission to find their victim. Quite a few mimicked the sound of shattering glass when fighting, whilst others just used their eyes to talk.

I read to them slowly, enunciating each letter. It was arduous but it was brilliant especially when they started to say their first words.

As the children grew I realised I would need recruits.

I had observed this world for a while, the demands of desire and what it would drive people to do. The lack of life on the streets, the lack of pride in the face of limited purpose. I assessed the gaps in desires, I sat with those who were quiet, those who drank themselves into a stupor.

I asked all of them if they could have all they wanted and why they were sitting here? The answer was overwhelming. A lack of meaning in their want, they didn't gain anything from doing what they wanted because it wasn't really what they wanted to do. There was no sacrifice in their desire, it was all too easy.

Some spoke of the Faceless and how they were holding them back by deliberately destroying what they had created or not appreciating their efforts. Others said they loved the Faceless, it appreciated their talents and applauded them for pursuing them.

Some said their Faceless had lied to them for years, telling them they were good before they performed their passion in front of their friends and a few laughed. They kept pursuing their passion but always felt frail to the fiction of it all, finding more and more friends over the years who would laugh through clenched jaws as they performed.

I could feel Osbourne's Liberation war happening again, but this time violence was venerated.

These people, these drinkers, these non-thinkers, they had no guidance. I could give that to them. I started thinking about what guidance meant.

I considered everything I had read, some worlds seemed to have structure, a certain outline to follow for harmony to prevail. Then I found one excerpt about the need for order in a world full of desire. About the why behind it all, why people were passionate, why they pursued a particular interest as if they had something to do it meant their lives mattered.

People had forsaken the why and how of it all and just focused on the what and when; what they wanted and when they would get it.

I ripped this out and stuck it to my wall. I annotated it, questioned it, and used it as a script for the new world:

Meaning Manifesto:

Humanity used to matter more than our individualistic desires. One hundred years ago we were at war with each other over the demands of our wants. There were those who wanted and won and there were those who wanted and lost. There didn't seem to be a logic to it, it was just luck. This luck led to bloodshed and loss.

Selfishness walked through the flames, stronger and bolder than before. People feasted on its body, consuming its strength and in it they found survival.

The creation of the Faceless aided this. Initially designed to help us with the aftermath of the war, to repair our destruction. They learned how to build our cities back, they created our communal sleeping sections so everyone could have a house.

After we stood looking up at the pillars they had perfected for us, we decided we could use them for our own gain, manipulating them so that they would adhere to the demands of our desires. They have let us lead lives of lies, taking over our minds, I have watched as we slowly start to die.

A mirage of musts seduced, and our desires deceived, both allowing us to believe that our demands should be met simply because we wish for them to be. We have placed too much value on ourselves whilst forsaking everybody else. There are those with passions who are pushed down because we no longer value them, their skills do not serve to enrich our lives, so we ostracise them.

Your happiness is a mere mask on the face of neglect, the instant gratification you call success has not been worked for but killed for. It is self-sacrifice and fulfilment that truly feeds the soul itself; the very creation *born into origin to aid our survival is what is killing us.*

Success happens slowly, the process developing over time. This allows the individual to truly feel the full impact of their talent, of their skill, absorbing its benefits and then seeing them applied to wider society.

Life is not meant to be easy, but it is also not meant to be about suffering. Look at you, you are suffering. We have created a world in which we are crushed by the pressure of possibility, producing impossible pedestals for those who pursue passion.

Of course, there are those worthy of that position but there are also those who are not. Who have we let determine this? A robot hive that steals the means from our minds. In my world we will all have a Basi, it is called pride and we will earn it through production.

Success is the smile on the faces of the many, it is not the smile that stands up high and alone whilst the world burns beneath them.

We see these statues of success that do not share our face and we think why not me? Your entitled existence is rendering you into an echo, your anger pushing you further away from seeing yourself in stone. But who deserves to have this legacy anyway? Especially when we are all killers.

Look at your hands, at your knuckles, feel the weight in your stomach, does that make you human? Does that hurt make you who you are? Does the harm you inflict on the face of another feel good?

We all share the same story, we just wear different faces. So put your drinks down, relax your fists and outstretch your hand, learn to love again, learn to heal, and learn to help others to do the same.

The glorification of violence, walking away with someone else's blood on your hands, does not make you a victor, it makes you less than others. The act itself removes your essence of humanity. When you look at the blood, when you look at the body, do you not see your own story, those final seconds before eternal emptiness? Do you not see what you have truly done?

To always want can culminate in failure, leading people to drink, take drugs and bring about the deaths of others. We justify this barbaric act as deserved just because there is no one to tell you this is wrong, would you end your own life just as you have ended theirs? Are you deserving of death just because no one has said you are not?

It is not deserved, death is never deserved.

You were not born wanting to be a killer, you were not born wanting to hurt so why do you do so now? You must know who you are not before you know who you are. You may have killed but you were not meant to be a killer, you may have become a drunk or a junkie, but you were not meant to be an addict.

No one is born wanting this, this is just what happens when you do not achieve what you primarily wanted. I can take you back to that first hope, that first dream, and together we can achieve it.

Our children, once a cherished addition to our lives, are now left on the roadside to rot. We once knew the word 'family' but now I fear we have forgotten its meaning. There are gaps in our adult numbers, an abundance of absence and it is because we have abandoned our younger forces.

Hundreds of skeletal children, forced to huddle on the streets, because we do not want them in our sleeping sections turning to the same violence we champion in order to survive. We do not cheer when we see them, so little of us want to see them, so we don't, but we know they are there, we know it is our fault.

These fighters can become the foundation to our future success, but we have left them to feast on the bones of others just to call it survival. We can stop that, we can do better, we will teach them, we will take them in, we will give them purpose and make them prosper.

I have started to save the streets, I have nurtured children the way I had once wished to be held. I have taught them skills, with no famia to feed from. They have learned how to replicate the famia's food from the earth. Their voices, once incomprehensive whispers, are now eloquent and empathetic.

You have built a world where neglecting the creatures of your own creation is necessary for the sake of desire. In my world, neglect is not a known word and, instead, they thrive. You could thrive there too.

Whether we are creating something new, solving a problem, or providing a service, our production is a reflection of our commitment to making a difference. It is through our production that we leave our mark on the world, leaving behind a legacy that inspires others to follow in our footsteps.

Self-interest must be sacrificed for the greater good. To be the best you have to be part of something bigger than yourself. Our population is the army in the pursuit of passion. Our collective consciousness will make you more than you could ever be alone. Production is the tangible result of our purpose and pride in action. It is the outcome of our hard work, creativity, and dedication.

Together, purpose, pride, and production form the pillars of success and fulfilment. They empower us to lead with passion, integrity, and a relentless pursuit of excellence. Let us embrace these principles wholeheartedly, as we work towards a future filled with purposeful endeavours, genuine pride, and impactful production.

These are the values that will be instilled within all of those saved from the stress, all of those who become disillusioned with the Faceless. These are the survivors who will live to see a new world and see themselves smiling in it.

We will build structures to inspire the youth, these institutions will be called Discite, where they will learn to read, love to write and understand the power of a number.

These institutions will be run by the thinkers, the writers of our world, and the performers who know how to change, and how to captivate.

Sleeping sections will be available to all those who prove their production value is worthy of a personal building.

You will feel a sense of ownership in your life, you will be able to call what you have your own instead of just what was given, it will be rightfully yours instead of something that was demanded.

Life will follow a set routine, and no longer will precious hours of day be dead by our laziness, we will use all of the resources we have to dutifully define the hours ahead of us.

We will be greater through connection, overcoming isolation in the face of passion peril through communication, a united front conquering the hole within ourselves telling us to destroy who we are for we will never be good enough.

Find something meaningful, allow yourself to matter and join me. You will have the space for yourself, with two days a week to dedicate your drive to the demands of your own desires, satiating all aspects of humanity. You can be yourself but also be everyone else, spending the rest of the time cultivating a community and feeling connected.

We will become the family so few of you were able to have, we will nurture you and your goals. We will do all we want together, making sure everybody gets a fair shot at the life they want to lead.

For the creators, you will not only get to give the gift of inspiration, but your works will be showcased in public places called libraries where your books will be read by all.

Instead of pursuing one facet of the self, my world gives you the opportunity to pursue all. Our next generation will come to understand how to paint, how to read, how to cook, garden and build, fortifying the earth into fruition, and their skills will be supportive to the wider society.

Your tunnelled minds will collapse, and you will finally see the view. If you want to have your own, permanent, internal Basi you simply have to desire the demands of the following statements.

1. *A deserved death is not a recognised concept. To deliberately end someone's life is a callous act that will now on be known as murder.*

2. *Drinking is not a permitted passion, productive passions are to be pursued and celebrated.*

3. *You are not good simply because you want to be, you must try. Success comes through sacrifice.*

4. *Defy the Faceless who keep you small and sedated, defy their practices and promises and prove something of yourself.*

5. *To be saved you must save others.*

Our own limitless lives have led us to narrowmindedness, only seeing the self instead of our impact on others. By saving the many, you will save yourself.

I began handing my manuscript out, leaving it on tables in bars, on posters in the city, in the Liatrium and the Museum of Now. I found the penthouses and pushed it through the doors, knowing that my principles would be agreed to by others, I waited.

Chapter Twenty Seven

Florence

When something dies it does so in the dark, so I sentenced myself to the shadows and allowed myself to rot. My name was not ushered by the streets anymore, I had become a spectre haunting my life. Held captor by my capabilities.

I felt Tiana's eyes watching me from my bedside, she had been in this position weeks before she died, but she had hidden it better. She didn't speak to me, she just stared.

We had never really understood each other much in life, I had admired her, she had encouraged me, but it was her death that brought us closer. I started seeing us as the same. She was everything I could be, did I really want that?

There was a cave within me full of overlapping echoes, all screaming, 'why?' She had led us to a cliff face, promising the sights would be worth it and as we got a glimpse, she had stumbled down, no glamour in her final show, leaving us nowhere to go, an audience left in uproar with only themselves to shout at.

In my demise, their love for me had galvanised. Messages from friends flooded my Faceless, who would once a week usher out films I was requested to star in. Flattered yet overwhelmed, I shut them down. I wasn't ready to face who I would become if I kept going yet, I wasn't ready to determine who that face would look like.

Then one day, after a while of silence, my Faceless said there was a show about an underwater researcher, a role they had made specifically for me. With sweat on my clothes and a mat of hair I pushed my finger into my passion plaque.

'To act.'

"Is this right for me?, I asked my Faceless wiping my nose.

'Whatever you want is right for you.'

Tiana sat watching me as I said yes.

The show, Aquatic Antics, was aimed at children despite being categorised as a dark comedy series. It was set on the ocean floor and involved a lot of method acting, diving into deep salt pools, chanting some lines underwater and swimming for several hours a day. It was my last chance to be who I wanted, to reclaim my name.

I tried to enjoy the show, it aligned with so many of my morals, heralding resilience in the face of adversity and humour in the echoes of humiliation. It was harder than anything I had done before and I found the takes tiring, the exhaustion overtaking the purchasing points and the press tours. I wasn't being authentic, I didn't really want it anymore and it started to show. Tiana taunted me in the dressing room, only appearing as my reflection.

I still spent my downtime in the darkness, I had found ways to get my hands on coke, I told my Faceless to block all notifications from my friends, embarrassed to allow them to see me this way but not embarrassed enough to want to change.

Despite being signed for a 3 year running, the first series drowned, something about low audience ratings and demands. My desire dropped with it. Eva was relentless, rabbiting on about the oxygen cycle and the movement of energy through ecosystems.

She was supposed to be entertaining to little ones and her comedy titillating to parents but she was patronising, it felt as though she knew more than I did and she never stopped talking. Each day a reel of her script for one episode would be delivered, my mouth hosting 80% of screen time.

I heard her gargling voice swimming through my thoughts at night. She would possess me when I went on dates, her voice bubbling up after a glass of wine, spurting out facts about the continental shelf, describing the difference between the pelagic and demersal fish as my date would leave to the loo without ever returning.

She even entered the stage when I tried to deliver speeches at comedy award shows. At first I was called cute by the public for doing this little 'skit' and then it became 'creepy and unsettling'. I was embodying my character's persona 'too intensely', they said I no longer felt 'shore of myself'.

I sold my soul to this serpent. What happened to the serious acting, the grit, the intellect, the halo around your individual intelligence after stepping out of the screen?

Tiana sat with me as I watched my own burial. I had once been respected, now suddenly a badly written woman made me a bad actress and ultimately a bad person.

I would berate my passion plaque which told me this is still what I wanted. I knew it to not be true, I knew that this meaningless role was not a desire of mine but the demand to be seen again overtook it all.

I spent the next two years of that show slurring my script, too jacked up on cocaine to deliver anything inspiring. I gave up in the end, locking myself in my penthouse, injecting friends into my veins to stop the thoughts from spiralling, Tiana cheering me on.

I was exiled by the press, each report a seething remark on my delivery. They didn't care that I was on drugs, they cared that I didn't seem to want what everybody else dreamed of.

Eventually, some other young actress took Eva from me and handled her beautifully whilst I slept next to my own sick and cried into a glass square.

Tiana lingered during the interim of my existence. She only began to fade when I allowed myself to do small screenings again. I had a cameo appearance in Fishy Business, a cheesy sitcom about two lovers, Max and Sam, who inherit a mysterious goldish.

Spoiler alert! It turns out the fish is a man-eating alien that the two men try to keep secret until it has a feeding frenzy. I was lucky enough to be its first victim 'Woman on the phone'. I had a whole minute of screen time, half of which I spent screaming all while wearing an Eva T-shirt to add a bit more comedy at my expense.

I still wasn't off the drugs. They drowned out all the dreams that haunted me, all the days that went wrong. They soothed the silence, so it no longer felt as though the sound was spying on me.

In between the injections and the lines, on my blurry days full of festering faces and dizzying darkness, I forced myself out. I watched reruns of classic films, my favourite being Little Women, Marie Antoinette and an indie house movie called Four Good Days. These days were better, but they were fleeting.

I needed to get better but I didn't really want to.

Chapter Twenty Eight

Henry

The four of us banded together, still headed by the eldest girl, and trained by the eldest boy. I assumed they were older anyway, as they were both bigger and spoke more than the others.

We combined our passion points and bought some pods for the famia I had acquired. We had been eating better than usual for the past few weeks, there had even been enough of a break between fights that the wounds from them had begun to heal.

We had been allowed to smile, but you could not sip at happiness and expect it to last.

Gathered together under the fragile roof, the eldest girl declared it was time to head back to the bars. The capsules were running low, and we had had more than enough rest. She told us we were well enough, and the eldest boy consolidated this, commending our strength. I knew there wasn't much choice in the matter, and I wanted to please them. Agreeing meant food and a better chance at finding shelter; agreeing meant staying alive.

The bars seemed busier this evening, which meant more chance of us pulling a successful bet. With the few of us remaining the eldest two offered themselves up first. Initially, their offers were met with tuts or batting hands pushing them aside, not all of the drunks wanted danger, most of them wanted to escape it. But find a certain type in a certain mood and violence would ensue.

A tall, muscular man with a disappointing beer gut approached the eldest boy.

"You and your lot should leave here if you want to make it through another night, your type has no right to be in these places", he wobbled a little, trying to direct his finger to the boy who was biting back a laugh.

Unfortunately, the man sensed this and screamed at him, his fist landed squarely in his jaw.

Spitting out blood the boy whimpered "Mate, if you want a fight, someone needs to place a bet on who will win, otherwise I'm leaving, we have to eat."

"I do want to fight, and I don't think you'll need to eat after this", his foot hitting into the boy's leg, an audible snap echoing out as the bone broke.

No one reacted, they just continued sipping their drinks, having their conversations, and staring at the wall. I had to swallow the sick that had curdled in my throat. The eldest girl had started screaming, watching as this mountain pummelling further into him. The man threw him to the floor, and I watched him bleed to death from the comfort of my coward's corner.

He spat on his skeleton and looked up with a sly smile, watching as the eldest girl wiped her eyes and clenched her fists. She landed a good hit to his throat, which delayed his blows as he choked but only enraged him further. I turned away, too sickened by the scene to see anymore.

I was thankful at least that the youngest girl who had been with us, had gone, hopefully before witnessing too much of this, hopefully to some safer place. I heard a loud thud as the man cheered.

I turned to see the eldest girl's body falling to the floor like a pile of discarded clothes. I should have left but I was too scared to move, peering out behind a large wooden column as this man tore bystanders down from their barstools and ripped into them, only letting them fall when their bones had snapped, and their bodies resembled bags of blood. Like thunder and lightning, this man was a storm from which there was no shelter.

Some of his victims tried to fight him before meeting their demise, leaving his nose broken and his eyes bruised. An act met with cheers from the room who had now picked up their heads to watch, placing their drinks down as they did so. A few of the crowd clearly knew the mountain man cheering 'Mark' on as he went to fight another drinker.

Despite the glasses broken on his head, he continued, screaming victoriously as he pulled the shards from his 7th trophy. No one was attempting to stop him, but by now most people were scrambling for the exit, knowing they would be next. Soon it would just be the shield of the street between this man and me.

His hand's balls of blood and his face was green as he approached yet another person. I sprinted out of the city, holding my breath as the scenery changed to the sleeping section, turning my back only to see more houses. I choked on cold relief to realise that here there were only blue skies.

I had tried many times to get back to the sleeping section, but it had never appeared for me. Its fortunate inhabitants not wanting to see the consequences of their creations.

I knocked on a few houses to no answer, despite lights watching me and their TVs tuning me out. One man opened the door, saw me, and then slammed it shut. A woman maintained eye-contact with me as she drew her curtains. I was the unknown, I was the body of guilt, and no one wanted to look at me as I pointed at them with my frail form.

I tried a quiet house, one that, despite its identical structure, seemed smaller than the others, its colour fading. There was one light on and as I approached the door I could hear the TV mumbling. It was this house or heading back to the massacre in the city I had learned to call home.

Chapter Twenty Nine

Jill

Jackson and Joe were about to find out that they had chosen each other in the blind love challenge, everyone was holding their breath, blinking back tears elated to see the men unite. With all 6 contestants standing up, with Joe and Jackson in the middle, host Olivia opened the envelope. Just as she was about to break the silence there was a knock at my front door.

I continued watching, a quiet whoop and clap in the corner when Joe and Jackson kissed. "One more time for Joe and Jackson!", screeched Olivia. The knock turned her champagne cheers into watery whispers.

My eyes darted to the window, the grey blinds letting flickers of a small person into my lounge.

This was not Mark, so I continued watching my show, waiting for the mystery guest to be revealed but the knock came again. I struggled up from the sofa and slowly stepped toward the front door.

A meek, "coming", left my lips.

I opened the door to a mousy boy who had dirt around his ears, his mouth, on his hands and on his clothes. His eyes were frightful and full of tears.

"Please let me in."

I looked around and did so. He was silent for a while and sat shaking on my sofa. I brought him the famia and a blanket. After a while of chewing on warm chips and staring at the floor, he opened up to me.

He was called Henry, his parents had abandoned him, he had been hurt, he had been starved, he had done what he had to survive. He had offered himself up in fights, he had been the victor which meant ending lives to extend his own. He believed he was 14 but couldn't be sure how long the streets had swallowed him.

I thought of Grace, I thought of Emily and what the Voice would have made of her after I left. I asked him if I could hold him. He didn't know what that meant.

Gingerly, I approached him and pulled him into me, for a minute he was still and then he softened and sobbed. He was in floods of tears, gulping as he tried to stand up against each wave of life flooding his throat, a tsunami of wrong that he had been submerged in and expected to swim out of.

I ran him a bath, finding even warm water was too hot for him but he sat in it with the soap all the same.

I put my show back on. I turned it up then turned it down. I bit my nails, feeling my face as it fell into a frown. What was I meant to do with him?

Mark wasn't here and I had lost Grace and left Emily. Everyone that needed me I had let down, how would it be different with Henry?

I knocked at the bathroom door and told him that I would leave some clothes and the famia outside for him, that he was welcome to come down when he was ready or simply use my bed to sleep in instead.

He came downstairs in an ocean of oversized denim and cotton, smelling of mothballs and patchouli. He was eating chips with the steam still on them. He slept on the floor of the lounge as I fretted in bed. I knew Mark would come back and Henry could not stay.

In the morning Henry was gone, he had done my job for me. Sighing with relief, I walked into the kitchen to make a coffee before counting the birds. The backdoor was open.

I ran over to it, fists raised like when I would fight the Voice, but there was nothing, Henry was asleep on the floor, Mark's shirt wrapped around him.

I counted 12 chaffinch, 4 goldfinch and 3 starlings before he woke up.

Chapter Thirty

Florence

Rotting in the dark, my eyes swollen and sore from staring into empty spaces, my hands clawed from trying to clutch at fading memories. I sat pulling apart each thread of my life, trying to understand why the tapestry had been woven this way and what its final picture would show.

To be looked at in this world is to be known. I was a commodity, selling myself for a step up to the next pedestal. Everyone claimed they knew me. Visceral and raw, my body, my brain, my misplaced glare, my wandering eye, all captured and dissected, mosaics of myself made up my entire life.

After Tiana's death and my recent demise, I wanted to use my platform to change people's lives. But rather than inspire them to do as I had done, I wanted them to understand what was truly right for them, that their wants are not always what is good.

To the darkness I would tell the truth, that being known will not make everything okay, being plastered on a wall, be it in a beloved fan's bedroom, or framed in gold inside a museum, it will not make you feel whole. So if you're going to do something don't do it because you want to be known, do it because you feel it is what you're supposed to do.

You become scripted whilst everyone else is allowed to be opinionated and even when their arrows are aimed at you, you must smile and thank them for the attention. I had to say stuff like I was blessed and fortunate, that I was just a blueprint to base your life on, and that if you did as I did, we would be the same.

I was not privileged or blessed, I was here doing what I was supposed to do. You have to learn that you are no longer a person, you are a spectacle. I had to assume that even when I closed the door it would be made out of glass.

I didn't have the grace to make an awkward first impression, a human impression. I had to permeate perfection, all I could do was act with passion and wait to see what the Faceless made of me.

There was never a new day for me, never a fresh start. I was forced to wake up each day and wear the faces of yesterday, dressed in whatever I had said or had failed to say. When you are in the moment, that is all you have.

When you're facing a crowd, whose face do you search for if you're surrounded by strangers?

I was hired for exclusive events but when I showed up it was like the room had become a camera and I had to dance in front of it not knowing when the flashes would end. These fans, my 'friends', received a scripted version of me to ensure they kept liking me.

Even when they were crying, and shaking in the presence of their star, I had to comfort them with recycled lines from films or shows I had been in. I wanted to scream at them, I am you, I was you, please talk to me. They'll claim to know you but won't bother to take the time to ask about the stories you don't see on a screen.

Whispers become the loudest form of communication. The mumbles and mutters haunt you, a good word never follows a held breath.

I had only failed once before and I had tried to make sure it was my last. One of my first introductions to acting came when I was very young, but I was always ambitious, always tossing my skills to the next level, challenging myself to see how quickly I could catch up.

My friend had produced a small audience play before pitching her plot to be made into a film. I was only 12 so I had a minor part with a few lines and minimal appearances.

This would be fine. I had performed on stage before, I had been encouraged to do this since I showed signs of loving the spotlight as a child.

I had my 6 lines, I knew when they were, I had my velvet headdress, my overflowing skirt dress and faux gold jewellery. My first cue entering the vibrant garden set with only the lead, it was time for me to deliver my lines.

"I need for you as you love for me", I began, poised and strong.

I took a breath, walking toward the lead. I had to lower myself gradually as I got closer.

"I will desire you do nothing but that shall be what you do desire", I delivered perfectly.

I was close to her now, my knees almost kissing the ground. My headdress began to slip.

"And, girl though at times I have not shown you the love that you needed to see, one must know this is how it has always been."

 I took one step closer to her and tripped, my headdress falling over my face, the ruffles of my skirt tricking my toes disrupting their grip. Not only did I fall onto the lead, but I also fell off the stage, pulling her down with me.

This was the first time my mother had seen me act, it was the last show she went to. She had missed a big art opening that evening and I had let her down. My friend was unsuccessful when trying to pitch the play to the film Faceless in the audience. I hadn't been perfect so everything had gone wrong.

When I told my Faceless that I didn't want to embarrass myself like that again and that it was time for me to stop, they convinced me otherwise. They reminded me of how good I was at creating a scene, both telling a story and performing it with great depth and emotion.

My performance had been passionate and convincing, it was just my delivery that had let me down. To fail was to find an opportunity to do better so that is what I have done ever since, better.

I had been born into the spotlight and I had let it swallow me. Everyone wanted to see me sparkle, no longer a human being but a hook on which they could hang what they had failed to achieve, when I won they did too.

My passion plaque told me this is what I wanted as it scanned my eyes and measured my blood pressure, so I agreed to act, it was in my bones, it was in my blood.

But I had begun questioning how much I wanted this after all the late nights and early starts, after the strain in my cheeks from forcing a smile on my face, the shin splints tempting me to trip after years of wearing heels daily. I wanted to tell the stories, I wanted to be the star but I couldn't keep shining so brightly.

My Faceless must have sensed this as it attempted to assist me in my ventures, finding potential auditions and putting in recommendations for me. This led to increased alerts on minor roles in commercials or as a comedic cameo in a major movie. This notion led me to Eva.

Eva took this opportunity off me, she was not better, she stymied who I was meant to be and now I had to crawl back to where I came from to be born again.

Growing up I had been mesmerised by the stars in the shows I would watch with my family. Before my father left and my mother's art was recognised, it was a routine we had. My brother would come in after hockey and we would sit and watch shows together, taking turns to pitch our favourite sitcom or to recommend a film.

I always chose the story of the little girl with shiny shoes who gets waltzed off on a technicolour adventure where she can get all she wishes for and ends up wishing for home.

One weekend there was a power cut and it was my turn to choose so my brother and I acted out a film. I had written the script and told him how each scene would go and we delivered a tear-jerking performance.

Isn't that what I wanted, to be part of something meaningful again? To leave a lasting impact on a person rather than to be a fleeting 'thing' in their day, an irritating mute at worst and a jingle they sang at best.

But maybe not, maybe after years in the spotlight my eyes had begun to burn and my feet had started to tire, perhaps these slim pickings were all I needed now to feel satiated. I thought of people similar to me, Hazel whom I had not spoken to in over a year.

When I met her she had just landed her first breakout role in what would become a space trilogy yet now it was as though she had never existed.

I thought of Lola who had auditions after only managing to secure 2 semi-successful roles. She had become like Tiana now just without the popularity or publicity, no posing on the streets for passion points for her just slamming shots in a local grease joint waiting for her life to feel like something she wanted to be a part of again.

I thought of Jada who had it all and was so happy, she drank but not to a detrimental extent. She never had to sing a song unless she wanted to sing it, because she wanted to be herself and that is exactly who she was whereas I was still building those bricks back up again.

I had aged since my fan-made fabric dress, I had gotten larger since my first three films, I didn't have a romantic interest in my life, and there was nothing malicious or quirky about me. I could deliver a scene and I could go home.

Is that the person I wanted to be? In the low light all the glass bottles and pizza boxes, all the spilled pills and free clothes looked like mountains I would have to climb to reach myself again, I just needed the courage to give myself a hand to get over it.

I got an alert from my Faceless about an advert for a new famia. I decided to give myself one more shot.

Chapter Thirty One

John

Most people believe they are better than average whilst being below but I know I am better than average and my passion plaque could prove it. I am deserving after all.

Maternal Instincts was going to be made into an advert for the new famia, plot twist the vestiger dies of starvation because she had given up on her wants and couldn't afford the new famia.

Some people laughed at first when I shared this story, commenting on how they didn't realise I had written 'the one with the catchy jingle', whilst others nodded slowly and said that it was a 'really good 30 second story'.

So it wasn't a bestseller, the public didn't want that anymore, they wanted to consume delicacies, not fantasies. It wasn't true to my creative vision but it is something I had creative input on, something I had produced after years of silence and stagnation.

So maybe I am not in the museum and that is a bit annoying and maybe they removed the nuisances. But it was my story, it had been whipped and skinned, had its identity removed, but there it stood and oh how I loved it because I could call it mine.

My art would be known, witnessed by many and perhaps change their lives, if they purchased the new Famia at least. My mystery had been revealed in the final line 'Nothing mysterious about it, just good home cooking', the true secret to quality dining.

I increased sales for the product by 15% and got sent my own one. I put it on the shelf next to my books, a testament to my creative triumph.

Jada called me.

"Good to see you back where you should be."

"Back where I belong. I'm getting a Penthouse with it and having a party, bring yourself and your mates, it'll be a riot, famia 2 and sapphire margaritas on me."

I moved into the Penthouse, shocked to realise it was one of the smaller sizes, only having 7 rooms as opposed to Jada's which had 15. Checking my passion power, ashamed that I hadn't been too authentically happy about producing an advert, the soul stripped out of the story for commodity.

But here I was back in the room, with adoring fans and friends on the way. The world was finally rising with me, the sun existed for me.

I placed my books, now relics, torn and tired at the edges after hours of being digested, in pride of place on a marble column, encased in shimmering glass in the centre of the main room. I shaved. I showered. I smoked and I sparkled.

My guests were arriving.

Jada came with several long-legged friends. They were all beautiful and brilliant.

They were chatting about a new song coming out and the joys and jolts of choreography when I approached them.

Jada wrapped her firm arms around me.

"Like a satellite out in space, you have returned to your planet."

"How do you feel?", One of the girls, I recognised from a TV opera, asked.

"Powerful, deserved."

"Man, I love the jingle, did you write the jingle, that little trumpet at the end. So sick", said MILK.

"Well originally it started off as a novella but we all know that wouldn't have been successful but still, I wanted to try something. Essentially I provided the script and then the Faceless swapped it to this and look at how good it is."

Opera girl and MILK blinked with tight smiles whilst Jada nodded reassuringly.

"Who wants a drink? 6 Sapphire margaritas coming our way."

We didn't speak much about the advert after that, I played it on the big screen where it was met by a few drunken cheers and whoops.

Jada poured herself between groups. She was wearing an emerald green slip dress and silver heels, quite a simple look compared to some of the shimmering bodies sparkling in corners around the room. But still a spotlight seemed to shine on her wherever she walked, her large brown eyes and smile always dazzling.

Noticing the lull, she offered to sing some audience requests, which soon saw the whole room spinning with twirling bodies as I stood, smoking in the corner. This was my night, this was my story, and there she was stealing it with her song.

I switched off the speakers and ordered the Faceless to make people more drinks, to give out more of the new famias.

Soon people started making up excuses to go home, a couple of people took the famias but most said they had had a special one made specifically for a diet that suited them.

All these named people left feeling nameless. What did success mean to a star? I had been a spectre in my own spotlight, my stage stolen before I had stepped on it.

Jada lingered, spilt over the sofa, she was on her 7th margarita, the opera girl, who I now recognised as Anya, was talking about some vocal exercises and pastilles that she should try, whilst MILK snored. Florence, who had starred in the advert as the mother, perched on the side, her head on Jada's shoulder.

"Everyone feeling alright?", I asked.

Jada hummed happily, nodding her head for the rest of them. Florence blinked up at me.

"What was the story meant to be?", she asked.

"What do you mean?"

"Well, you said the Faceless twisted it to be more successful, what did *you* really want it to be?"

"Would you read it if I showed you the original document?"

Jada spluttered and Anya chimed in .

"Of course she wouldn't, no one has time for that now. I get bored after one page of lines on set and sometimes ad lib", Jada playfully smacked her shoulder as if she had just confessed some trade secret.

"Yeah, John you are the best but I gotta' say I prefer writing my songs than reading words."

Florence looked up at me. Big green eyes and lines stretched into her forehead.

"I suppose I would give it a try although I would prefer to hear it from you. Would you share it with us?", she said.

I downed another margarita and went to the backroom, hearing Anya saying that she was bored and wanted to go home for Jada to say, "Look, hear him out and then we'll go."

I sat back down with them, next to Florence with the original manuscript in hand. I read aloud from it.

"Wait, the mother did it?", said Anya.

"No way, no way. I could have sworn it would be the boy on the bike, but the mother omg that is mad", Jada replied.

"No it makes sense, the mother did it to ensure that her daughter made her first case a successful one", Florence explained.

'Incredible, incredible", applauded Jada.

"Cool story, shame about the advert that became of it", yawned Anya as she tapped on her phone, "You ready Jada?"

"Yeah, Flo you coming?"

"Oh, I'll be leaving in a bit I will see you later."

"Oh okay, see you later."

The girls left, shaking MILK awake and dragging him outside. Florence stayed very still and very quiet.

I got her some water and she took a painless pill.

"Are you good?", I said as I slammed down next to her.

"Do you ever feel like we are being lied to?"

I felt the floor beneath me rumble, she had just uttered something I had thought for years but always felt unable to say.

"In what way?"

"I have always wanted to act, I have been a successful actress, I have also been a failing one. For a while it all felt as though it was meant to be, every day made me happy, every day I felt alive and now I feel lost, I feel all that I wanted no longer wants me."

"I feel this way too, I feel I was once told I was capable of writing world's into reality and now I cannot form a sentence without screwing it up."

"I think I got to the highest point possible and then realised there was nothing now but the descent, so that is where I went."

"I didn't even reach the top. I tell myself I did, I tell myself I once made it so I can do it again, but I never really made it, maybe momentarily but what is a moment to someone that lives life at the top?"

She gazed at me with wet eyes, analysing my features. She was pretty, younger than me by a good few years. She looked like moonlight, always waiting to be seen by the sun.

"I noticed your other books, could you read me one."

So I read through the synopsis of each one, navigating her through 20 years of my life starting with Synthetic Skies, a young adult novella heralded as brave, controversial, and contagiously good, it was broadcast on the Basi for three weeks.

Then of course Stellar Chronicles. My magnum opus, three stories, following Star-seer Sarah Davis who discovers stardust particles which possess extraordinary properties, granting individuals temporary superhuman abilities.

"Drawing energy from the stars themselves, the Stardust becomes a catalyst for both wonder and chaos", I continued to explain.

"That one, read that one."

So I took her on Sarah's quest to understand the nature of Stardust, telling her how this led Sarah to join a covert intergalactic organisation known as the Starfinders.

Alongside her eclectic team of experts, including a fearless pub fighter and a brilliant alien archaeologist, Sarah ventures into uncharted territories encountering alien civilizations and perilous challenges at every turn.

As Sarah delves deeper into the secrets of the universe, she uncovers a hidden agenda—a powerful, clandestine group known as the Consortium which aims to harness the Stardust's limitless power by doing so they would destroy entire civilizations.

As I closed the book after the first 5 chapters I said "On the Basi for 6 weeks. Written as an adult adventure book, it was the bestseller of sci-fi for 2 years, 20 years ago."

She nodded, "Can I take a copy to my penthouse?"

I was spinning, the sapphire margaritas filling my throat. Someone wanted to read my writing, my words, my worlds. I went to the back room, threw up and grabbed her a separate copy. Signed it and then handed it to her.

"Thank you."

"Let me know what you think."

Then she went home.

As the door closed I looked around the room, pizza boxes from an order I hadn't eaten shrugged in corners, smashed glasses and spilled liquor decorated the walls and there were cocaine smudges on my glass coffee tables and marble kitchen surfaces.

My Faceless was busy trying to conceal this mess from me, but to me this was not a mess, this was the art of a party.

Gazing from the window, the starfish streets of the city sparkled for me. It was all so much that it didn't feel enough.

It was Florence that had made my night, made my life mean something in that moment. It had been 20 years since I had published any words and she was the first person that wanted to read them.

I moved out of the penthouse and back into the sleeping section a week later, never one to stay too long in a place I didn't belong.

Her illicit words swirled in my head and made space for more stories. This was not the time to succumb to the pressure of possibility, this was the time to pursue.

Chapter Thirty Two

Jada

I sat at the top of it all but I wanted to go higher. I told my Faceless of my thoughts, only needing them to arrange it all for me. I hadn't been on the Basi in a while and I needed something unbeatable, something that would secure me a spot in the sky, in people's minds for centuries.

I knew I was talented but I had to remind everyone else of this, I had to constantly outdo each performance to prove myself.

The starfish streets of the city below me, dazzled in their evening wear. Illuminated from the thousands of tiny spotlights shining up from my fans, I smiled as I prepared to sing the first note sung from 5000 feet.

I was sitting in a swing tied to a helicopter, stilettos strapped to my feet, my dress stuffed with thermal patches, though I didn't feel the cold or the wind, although I knew it had to be there. All I felt was the love from below and the power in my lungs. I was exhilarated as my voice boomed from beyond me.

Breathy and light, I sounded higher than usual, hitting new notes, and getting a different reaction from the crowd. Faces startled, an audience in awe of me.

I swung to and fro', titillating the crowd with a possible fall but hitting every note, with every word I wowed. As I was lowered 500 feet with each song, the sky falling around me, I maintained my smile and wide-eyed look, wanting to win the demands of my fans, to be a spectacle, to make a statement. I wanted to give them my glory as I plummeted a little further to the ground after every beat drop.

At 15ft I dropped my earpiece and used the wires from the swing to somersault myself back to the ground, landing on the heels of my stilettos. It was an impossible display of perfection that sealed my reputation as a superstar.

Not only would I be on the Basi, I would become it, an embodiment of all that it stood for, my performance immortalised in the Museum of Now.

I couldn't be topped, I had outdone myself. My schedule is filled with interviews, awards, and shows. I would frequently perform from helicopters or from submarines, always wanting to shimmer and continuing to do so. This is what I wanted and what I would continue to do.

I didn't need my passion plaque anymore so I got rid of it. I could see my talent reflected in the eyes of all those who screamed for me and that was all I wanted.

Chapter Thirty Three

John

"Art is never wrong", said the museum guide, "It's just art, never to be consumed as is, always to be mulled over. Each piece is a reflection of the creator's soul, a physical product of their story."

"How do they know what story it is they want to tell?", I asked.

Despite being wired to know how to answer questions I could tell this had caught the Faceless off guard, hesitating for just a moment as it loaded a pre-set answer most applicable to this.

"Writers often draw inspiration from their experiences, whether to create a specific message or fuelled by a certain character or setting. They may explore topics that resonate with social issues, aiming to encourage thought and emotion in their readers. Ultimately, the decision relies on the writer's personal perspective and creative vision. You don't always know what story you want to tell but if you have one in you, you will find it if you want to."

70 passion points for this. I didn't want philosophy, I wanted solutions and 15 minutes into a 2-hour walking tour my question list was only growing.

"This piece is particularly unusual, renowned as controversial by some but celebrated for its spirit by most."

We had stopped by a particularly large painting full of colourful splats in the silhouette of the woods I often walked through. How could someone look at something so beautiful and transform it into a beast?

"The artist would dunk live birds into different coloured inks before hurtling them at a large canvas. Of course, most of the little creatures didn't make it but 15% of her proceeds went to conservation."

It wasn't even impressive. It was just cruel.

"So I have to be different to be celebrated?"

"You can be like everyone else but that in itself would be quite a challenge as everybody is different."

"What if I am like everyone else? I enjoy the TV maybe a bit too much, I use my Famia maybe a bit too much, I don't know enough but claim to do so. I want to be good but fear I will never be."

"Then maybe that is your story, and if that is what you want it to be, why is there anything wrong with that?"

The Faceless took me to a different room full of clothes including a collection made from rust and a dress made from eyelashes that the creator had pulled out during times of stress.

"As you know the museum transforms every 6 months, refreshing its exhibitions with new ones but we always have our archival collection. Two rooms where we display everything from the past 3 years and then our catacombs which is everything ever. To explore them, that is 45 passion points."

"What do you mean everything ever?"

"Everything ever, if you want to see everything ever that will be 45 passion points."

I was taken to a regular-looking room. It was perhaps 25 by 35 feet and the only thing it contained was a glass panel and a large armchair, everything else was empty space.

The glass panel, which was about 3 metres away from the door, let you search for anything that had been featured in the museum.

Names were being added by the minute so I clicked on a random few to get my bearings. Writer Felicity Snorthirops appeared in the large space, she was sitting at her desk, undisturbed by my presence as she scribbled and scrutinised her stories.

Her best-selling book ,'The Many Masks of Me', is about a movie star who was convinced she was all the characters she played, blurring the boundaries of fiction and reality.

After a while she walked away, leaving the space blank again so I found a new face to fill it.

Rene Duchamp, an artist who painted circus performers behind the tent, had no mother and his father was an alcoholic acrobat. He sat behind the tent in front of me, his head deep into his sketchbook.

Emilia Rinaldi, a maverick in the realm of fashion design used broken famias and frayed wiring to create her pieces.

She recycled the thrown away to make it beautiful by incorporating picked butterfly wings and fresh vines into her sculptures, both of her parents are renowned in the fashion world and also previously featured in the museum.

They stood, slightly faded, just behind her shoulders watching her create with a quiet, but proud smile on their faces.

I am not sure how long I spent in that room, searching for some reassurance in the past of big names. Each had their own story, most with their names already made for them or their story handed to them on a broken plate. There was no one with a name or life like me. No cure for normality.

I retired after the 200th face. The eyes of giants do not usually meet the ground. I walked to the exit by a queue of people trying to find themselves in the faces of ghosts.

It was then that I noticed Jada was on the wall, one of her recent escapades immortalised behind glass, her latest song on a dial you could tune in to. A few of her friends had their own exhibits, noticeably smaller than hers but still up there. I knew she was good, I couldn't say the same for them but I knew I wasn't up there.

Despite my previous success, I wasn't in the archives, I hadn't made it into history. I knew I had to figure out how to.

I sat down in the visitors centre, the scenery was as opulent and the coffee tasted good but I somehow felt unworthy of its flavour, as if my presence was an insult to this institute.

I had no anchor to my own land, just the frame I was trapped in. I had nothing keeping me here but nothing to make me stay. I would never be one of the greats, I wasn't even enough for myself, had it all been a lie? How could I have written like I once had?

Before I left, I found a thick document on the floor, it was crumpled and stained with a few muddy footprints but something about its misfitted way drew me to it.

It read; *'Humanity used to matter more than our individualistic desires'.*

I spent the afternoon scouring through the writer's words, questioning what sort of world they were creating and where I stood in it. Which world did I prefer, the one I was used to or the one that promised difference, the one that promised success?

I thought of the words I had scrutinised, I thought of my story and my script and how it had been reduced to an advert that had no real relevance to the reality it was born from. I hadn't been included in this world's history but perhaps I could make it into another.

Chapter Thirty Four

Florence

A few weeks after John's party I had flicked through the pages of his book. I felt as though my own passion had become Sarah's consortium, stealing my power, and pushing me down.

The Famia advert had been fun to do but if I could have played true to the story, if I could have delivered the mother the way she should have been portrayed, I would have found meaning in this mess that my life had become.

I did not see the mother, as she had been written, as a monster, she had been misunderstood, wanting her children to do well, and stopping at nothing to provide for them.

I realised, without consulting my passion plaque, that my want had never been to act, it had always been about finding meaning, seeing the stories in the characters I had to play, and using my passion as a platform that they could perform on.

I thought about the conversation I had had with John, half mist now due to the rain of alcohol showering on my brain. I remember the relief as I let my words drip from my fingertips, I remember the recognition on his face, the reassurance that somebody else felt this way too.

My Faceless, busy gathering up the mess I had made over the months that I had finally permitted it to relieve me of, buzzed with a message. Jada was out celebrating another success. I wondered what success meant as I rubbed at my eyelids, which were swollen from staying up late.

I had no glam Faceless team here and didn't want to disturb mine so rubbed some concealer under my eyes, dragging a mascara brush through my lashes. Only knowing what to do from watching but realising how awful I looked after doing it myself, I scrubbed it off and opted for large sunglasses and a larger hat as a substitute for my on screen beauty.

The space shifted in front of me and I stood metres away from a champagne bar. I could already see Jada, MILK and Anya all laughing in the window, waving to me as they spotted my hat.

In that moment we all sparkled together, all praising our recent success. I knew my advert appearance made no mark on Jada's aerial performance but she didn't make this obvious.

I spoke to them a little about my sadness at not being who I once was. They all reassured me that I would get back there, but I couldn't tell them that I didn't want that. I couldn't tell them that what plagued me the most was my apparent lack of passion. The thing I had wanted had forsaken me, how could these shiny people ever understand that?

As the humdrum conversation of how their lives were ever evolving, how their passion plaque seemed to be malfunctioning or what passion they were currently pursuing swam over my simmering silence, I let my ears wander off into whispered conversations.

In the booth next to us there was a sharp looking man with a thick beard and lines around his eyes. He looked suave in his green suit and acted insistent, gesticulating at some out of view recipient.

"You have let your drink define you", he said.

I leaned backwards to see who he was talking to, ensuring he wasn't a madman speaking to walls.

The man on the receiving end was red in the face, folded into himself with his chin on his knees. He was quite young but his skin was sagging, as though trying to run away from the bones it was stuck on. He was shaking the glass he had been sipping on so frantically I could have sworn the ice would smash its way out.

Despite his trembling recipient, the emerald man spoke calmly and slowly, each word delivered with purpose and weight.

"You have let something that does not sleep define your dreams."

The trembling man had paused his shaking, he returned to sipping and began wiping his eyes with his free hand.

Finishing the glass he pushed it away, a gesture that said he knew liquor could not remedy him now. The emerald man seemed to be offering him a choice, he could stay there and be this mess or he could join him and be the man he was always meant to be, he could be meaningful, all he had to do was deny himself his current desires and join him.

The man reached for his glass again, a gesture that slumped in on itself confessing that nothing could and the emerald man understood this, nodding slowly before patting down his suit and getting up to leave.

He turned to see me staring, my head full of questions I could not verbally form. He nodded at me, as he opened the door and I felt the word 'wait' leave my mouth.

I do not recall if this disrupted my friends or if they continued sipping and sharing stories from different chapters in their success. The man paused.

"What have you offered that man?", I asked, pointing at the eyes staring into an empty glass.

He looked at me blankly, assessing what I was wearing, perhaps trying to place me.

I took my sunglasses off, "You just offered that man something, he said no. What was it?" I was aware of the desperation in my voice but too determined to let this go I stared back at him.

"I know you, you're Eva. I'm Will."

I shuddered. He sensed this, smiling as I recoiled.

"I think you have a party you're missing out on", he pointed back to Jada.

I didn't turn around, I felt myself sitting down in the closest vacant seat and gestured for him to join me.

He laughed a little, clear wrinkles in his cheeks appeared as he did so.

"You have let something that does not sleep define your dreams, you said that to him, what did you mean?"

"You do not appear to be an addict, you have barely sipped your champagne, you do not have a hollow gaze about you, you do not need my services."

"You don't think I am an addict, but you know I was the voice of Eva? Do you not know they replaced me with someone else because I locked myself in my Penthouse? Just because I look golden does not mean I feel the warmth of the sun."

He chuckled at this. "You don't understand the real reason behind the failure of your show, do you? Too distracted by all of the other stuff that hides the holes in life you don't want to see. You have all you want, all anyone wants, connection and recognition." Again he gestured to Jada and MILK.

"I would be wasted on you."

I was confused, the show had failed because I hadn't wanted it, my lack of authenticity had caused the ratings to drop. I shook my head, embarrassed now that I couldn't see properly from the hot tears in my eyes.

"I am yearning for something, I feel I have been searching for something else, something larger than myself for years. I am sick of skinning myself just to be seen, I just want people to look at me and see who I am instead of the characters I play."

He stared harder at me then. "What is it you think I offered that man?"

"Meaning, right?"

"And you don't have that?" He was standing up again.

"No, I thought I did but it's never enough."

He stopped and turned with a slow smile, "I, can't give you meaning, you have to find that for yourself."

I looked at the guy slumped in the booth again, noticing now how bloodshot his eyes were, how thin his body was, and how he had already ordered another drink.

"Do you want me to become him?", I whispered. "Will you help me then? Because trust me I am on the brink of being that every day, I have had other addictions, I have been led by a desire greater than my own demands and it is called darkness. I cannot help myself when what I want is bigger than what I need."

From inside his coat he produced a folded parchment. "If you agree to these principles perhaps we will become more acquainted."

I took it from him, reading the only visible line.

"Success is the smile on the faces of the many, it is not on the smile that stands up high and alone whilst the world burns beneath them."

When I looked up he had gone. I went straight from this interaction to my penthouse, despite a few concerned messages from MILK it seemed my friends had not noticed my departure.

Will's words weaved a world of purpose, one that promised to transport you from a product of your desires to a person who could be proud.

There was reward in sacrifice instead of just guilty indulgence, there was a chance to get credit where it was earned rather than where it was wanted.

I thought back to all of the faces I had worn. Sat in hair and makeup, happy to be made up as mad or ugly, or older or prettier, I wondered who I would look like if I was just allowed to be myself. A forgotten face, a meddled with mirror, always mocked me as I tried to forge my own identity.

I had come to see my features as a palette for someone else's existence, my body merely carved through the eyes of someone else's story. I was a plane for people to perform on. To all of these people - I had become faceless.

This manuscript ensured my desires would have promise if they could bring progression.

I had always delivered a convincing performance throughout my scenes, each act a further betrayal of my true identity as I allowed the character to take over completely.

Unruly and unleashed I let go of myself as I saw these lifeless ghosts perform in front of me, no longer a thread of humanity left in their shells. Their bodies crawling about on screen, haggard by the person they could have been and holsted by the dreams they would not achieve.

I am sick of wearing the faces of strangers to impress uninterested eyes. I am tired of the people I have tried to be in order to stand on slippery stages. I want to be in charge of the direction, I want to shape lives instead of having mine moulded into contorting puzzles.

Chapter Thirty Five

Henry

You could not trust the silence on the streets. It was fragile and fleeting, it meant there were eyes on you, it kept you on the move. Silence was a gun, always aiming at you from the shadows.

Here, at Jill's house, silence moved slowly, disrupted only by the shuffle of slippers, the song of bird or the flicker of fictitious TV. It was an echo of a world I had once been a part of, a world robbed from me by loud demands that I was deaf too.

Jill didn't need me to be anything, she simply allowed me to be who I was, to be present, to breathe. She was often fretful and anxious, frequently allowing her eyes to flitter to the front window and back but for the most part she acted grateful for my company. She let me know I was wanted.

It took a while to sit on her sofa and not feel stiff, it took a while before I allowed my skin to sink into its new surroundings. I always woke up worrying that it wasn't real, that the man in the bar had wounded me into a delusion but then, I would see Jill, smiling in her dumpy armchair as she counted the birds and I knew he was not here and I was safe.

I sometimes worried, after being there for a few weeks, that Jill would leave but she never did, her thin frame a permanent dip in the sofa or crunch in the armchair.

I had always been quiet but Jill didn't mind it, not prying too much when I offered single word answers to her questions. I was polite enough and she was happy for someone to smile with.

I felt hollow and transparent, not wanting to tread too heavily or chew too loudly. Jill gave me the Famia but I didn't want to be seen eating from it, so she always offered me her portion.

I craved her love but did not want to make my existence known, happy spending silent hours in an empty room, or sitting in the corner trying to make sense of the shows she watched.

At first, I didn't sleep easily either outside or on the sofa. Everywhere felt too much, I didn't deserve the softness of its touch but I was so tired. So tired and bitter that I didn't burn like the stars that defied the dark of the night and instead just felt like the abyss intent on swallowing their light.

This pain was perpetual, it would one day become my crutch as I tried to cover baggy eyes with a faint smile, forcing teeth over the sadness. I knew it had impaled my heart, taking all of its ability to love normally. So I stayed safe and stayed alone, only allowing myself close to Jill.

My pain had become my personality, the problem defined me but I used my voice to deliver it eloquently so that instead of discomfort people felt empathy. In those cold, echoey moments, when my body shivered on the streets or clenched in Jill's house, I could not have known the arms that would one day comfort me.

Jill was the first, and like a feral cat, I slowly let her love me. I would hold a mirror up to silence and shatter its shroud, throwing off its hand on my mouth and standing up proud. For now, I was understanding how to settle again, allowing my bones to relax.

Sat with Jill in the kitchen, counting the birds, I was captivated by their sound. There must have been birds on the streets but I had never heard them sing this way. Their songs so beautiful, their melodies shimmering in the sunlight. There was the rhythm in Jill's voice as she counted them and there was the beat in my heart as I smiled at this scene.

There was music again and how I held it in my head so loud, this noise was the sound of being alive and I would one day soon hope to dance to it.

Chapter Thirty Six

Mark

Each dark and light ended and began the same way, with me slumped upright, my chin drilling into my chest, feeling the constant flow of heavy alcohol lulling me to the edge of a wayward sleep.

My head, an anchor dragging my eyes to the ground, my hands rigid with pain. I was both empty and heavy, weighed by the wishes of a few lights ago that now settled in my sore stomach. I felt sober and sick and knew I needed a drink.

A few hours later I stumbled out of the bar, the sun shot through me, a golden dagger of light, a sudden ache to step back inside but the abyss of guilt gnawed at me, propelling me forward.

I looked at my knuckles and knew I had been a bad husband, Jill had her flaws but she was not a bad wife. I noticed my face in the window as I wobbled out, it was bruised and swollen and I knew I had been a bad person,

I had done something I hadn't wished to do and it had hurt so many, I didn't want this angry man inside of me but I had no other place to put him.

I would go home, confess, but quietly to cover up the extent of my mishaps, and she would take me back, she would make me good again. I didn't even need her to leave the house anymore, I could stay in with her, away from the world and we could stay safe together.

I would do better, then I would cut back on my drinking, having the occasional sip and occasional sniff to frame reality rather than mould it.

I had a benzo and pushed through the sticky breeze of summer. I struggled to find her sleeping section, getting more and more frustrated by every false face that came to the door. Then there she was, a silhouette in the doorway, her eyes blinking up at me.

"Where have you been?"

She was shaking.

Where was the ovation, where was the admiration? This is not the Jill I had once known, her arms no longer thrown around my neck and her kisses no longer on my cheek.

"Does that even matter? I am back now aren't I? Come on, come here, you have missed me, haven't you? God Jill, I missed you so much."

She stood still, her eyes full of fire.

"You have been gone for a year, Mark. You reek of urine and beer and sweat. I know projects take a while but what is this, I haven't seen you like this before?"

Then, I noticed a boy, a young lad, standing up from my sofa. He was wearing my clothes, his green eyes pinned on mine, his hands balls of fear.

I grabbed Jill, and pushed her into the wall, her back making a loud thud as it collided with the brick.

"You found someone else eh? Where is he then, where is the bastard's father, not man enough to face me?", I started yelling up the stairs.

"Get off me, get off me Mark!"

"I leave for a bit, to make you proud, to produce something beautiful for this city and you slink off with another man, looking after his son? You think you're loyal? Leave the house for other men but never for me." I spat in her face, "disgusting clump of woman."

She was biting into my knuckles now, her leg jutting into my stomach. I was spinning. My head heavy on my body so I stumbled as I let go of her and grabbed the boy.

Holding him by his shoulders I yelled, "Who are you then? Think it's alright to just invade another man's space, come on who are you?"

The lad spat at me, surprisingly strong as he pushed against my weight, his fingers launching toward my eyes, and landing a punch on the right one. I buckled for a moment, biting my tongue to stop myself from screaming.

My adrenaline weakened by the weight of the drugs I was under, I struggled to regain my stance. He kicked me in the shin as I reached for him again.

I managed to scramble back up, landing a weak punch into his stomach that caused him to double back.

Jill was screaming.

"Jill I am and always have been the man of the house", I spat up blood, laughing to see the red on my fingers, "whoever this kid belongs to needs to show his face now."

"It is not like that Mark."

I grabbed the kid again, I raised my fist just as Jill screamed, "Leave him alone, Mark."

Something shattered on my head.

Her figure shielding the boy's as I darted toward the ground gripping the side of my head.

"I know you haven't been at the projects Mark. I know where you have been and you'd best go back there", she said calmly.

Her face was fragmented, a hundred tiny Jills stood over me wearing a stern face as my head swirled in and out of sound.

"I have always been loyal to you, Mark. I would have waited for you even if it meant I only witnessed sunsets and sunrises until my final hour. I would have stood by you knowing there was not a version of you in this life that would do the same for me but doing so anyway because I loved you. But this version, this beer-filled, bruise covered angry man, I do not think can be loved by anyone. So get out."

"You couldn't even leave the house Jill." I choked over my own tongue spitting this line out and laughing at her.

Then four arms were around my legs and arms. My body was reduced to a ragdoll, her and the boy dragged me out of the door, where she stepped one foot out to kick me.

I lay there for a while. My head still bleeding but I felt at peace, an uneasy sense of still anchored me to the stone slabs of my previous life, my previous love and a different man's wife.

The dull groan of drowsiness drifted over me and I took out my flask to prevent my eyes from falling. Sipping, I stumbled upwards and away from the woman who could have saved me but didn't believe I was worthwhile anymore.

I went back to the bar, it was possibly a different one each time but it didn't matter, what mattered was the drinks kept coming and the drugs kept being taken.

I sat with a couple of cheery fellas I had met at least once before, their faces were yellowing and creased but they put it down to a good time. I didn't participate in their joy, I just ordered more rounds.

By the third, we were all jostling each other about, having a good fist fight. I went to order another round and the Faceless server blurted "Insufficient funds".

Unbelievable, I was a passionate guy. I walked to see my wife, I drink every day. I am a passionate man.

I laughed it off and hit the thing with slight force "It's probably just had liquor spilt on it", I slurred trying to get 6 shots of Bourbon again.

"Insufficient funds", the thing bleeped.

"My man, my man this one is on us let us get these, man you're a great guy we will get these."

So they did and we downed them and the sweet fire of success sat smiling on my face, but it didn't last. These were no longer my drinks and the men I was with had brought over women, women who didn't want to see me despite being teased into it.

I couldn't offer them drinks or drugs, so I showcased my bruises, a trail of triumph on my body. I sat explaining the story of each. The girl's whooped. Everyone in here loved a bar fight, I was still a legend after my last one, bringing the deserved death to 7 people.

As I get to the bite mark on my hip some guy promises me he will give me another to talk about if I let him have the first punch.

The angry man within me was growing impatient, excited by the expectation of violence.

So this is how the night went on, blood and glass, guts and fists, blades and cheers to screams and fear. It always starts as a bit of fun, a bit of a fight, something to be done and then he takes over. The angry man takes the rage, swallows it as his stage and laughs as he beats his opponents into a red pulp.

He enjoys the fists pummelling into his stomach, as he smashes glass over someone else's head. It is not what I want, it is what he wants and in this moment he can have it all as he ends the lives of many for a moment of applause.

8 dead. A new record. Initially I was championed again, applauded, I was a warrior until they felt threatened by my presence instead of feeling impressed. Realising the blood was not what they

wanted, the anger was not what they wanted and they fled, leaving the angry man with nobody left but himself.

I lay in the blood that does not belong to me and see it as a bath to breathe in.

I am always with these bodies, they are the reason the angry man is still standing there watching. He is both my shield and sword and I cannot fight him.

Chapter Thirty Seven

John

I had seen Mark that night. I had wanted one drink before going home to try and write. Halfway through my first pint, I heard the glass shatter, I heard the commotion, the whoops and cheers and thought little of it.

More whoops as I sipped the last dregs of my pint ricocheted around the bar as Mark buried his fists into the face of a man, who promptly stabbed his shoulder with a broken beer glass.

I knew the room was full of chaos, fires, and fists, but I sat still, sipping at my pint. Some people were cheering it on, placing bets on how many people Mark would take out, whilst others were starting to leave.

As I sipped my second, the cheers turned to screams as Mark, a blurred twist of furious red and bitter anger, hurled his fists at women, stabbing their eyes with broken glass and digging beer bottles into their skulls.

Some spectators tried to rush in and pull him off but his drug-fuelled rage and their drink-infused haze made them as movable as the liquor in their guts to him.

Despite his strength and structure, Mark was wounded, a gaping hole in the side of his head had opened up, letting out scarlet rivulets of thick blood. His body had failed to tell him this as he continued his frenzy, shoving his foot into the chest of a drunken man laying cheerfully on the floor, claiming his territory, and calling it victory.

Will's words are an alert system in my head. *You were not born wanting to be a killer, you were not born wanting to hurt so why do you do so now?*

Will didn't know that it was rare people read, especially those in here. He had a solution to Mark's actions but when a solution isn't shared it just becomes part of the problem. Silence is also a weapon.

Before that night I had only known Mark through the perspective of Jill, who I had only met once, she had only really spoken passionately about him. From her I knew he was a progressive man, he was a strong and loving character who just wanted to provide.

Now I could see him clearly, as a violent try hard who pushed to prove his worth, tackling people off their pedestals to claim their space as his own, knowing he was not worthy of power but still feeling deserving of its. He was clearly passionate but only for himself.

I pitied him, this mountain of man was pathetic, how it wobbled in the slightest bit of wind, threatened to be toppled by forces much less mighty than it, using his fists instead of thoughts.

I sipped the final moments of the night and swallowed a new story. Leaving bloodied and bruised bodies behind I knew this man would become my masterpiece. I would speak to Florence and we would make Mark the man we needed him to be, the figurehead for the future.

I arrived at Florence's penthouse almost instantly after grabbing a pen and Will's document. My head bubbling with the buzz of beer and something beautiful. I burst through her door.

"I've got a new story for us. One you will actually want to star in. Read this", I threw the document at her.

She glanced at it for a few moments, silently scanning the sentences.

'This is Will's manuscript, he is a bit of an odd guy, seems detached but I've read this and I agree with him. What do you want to do with it?"

"He wants us to convince people to destroy the Faceless and to follow his way for our saviour. I don't know about you but I struggled to understand its entirety and *I* enjoy words, they are my thing but Will, he offers a different tongue. He wants change but isn't introducing it the right way. He doesn't know that it is rare to read here, he doesn't know that the drinkers are going to be too blurred to focus on this. And we all know what happens to words when we give them to the Faceless."

"Moving image", she whispered.

"Using this document, your acting experiences and the observations I have made, we can make this into a film that will speak to the masses, and the Faceless won't even know they have brought about their own downfall."

She locked her Faceless into a small cupboard and sat down beside me, she had advice as to how to create a convincing character.

'To captivate an audience you must have a sympathetic protagonist, one that holds up a mirror to the watchers."

I made Mark a man again. His visions of being a builder, a loving husband and a hero to his home all shone as badges on his lapel before each testament to his triumph became a catalyst to his own downfall. He had once truly loved Jill but he had always loved himself more.

This essence of him still existed in some quiet echo, with this film we could bring him back, we would bring back the encouragement we all needed to define ourselves.

I recalled the night of Mark's demented demise to Florence who saw him as a monster.

"No Florence, he is not a monster, he is a man, this is what anyone can be capable of given his set of circumstances."

Together we battled the conventions of humanity, hedonism, and innate selfishness as we gave birth to a complex character.

"They should be a woman, this character, so that I can play her. I can take ownership over myself."

"Yes and they should be someone who is struggling to find happiness in a world full of smiling faces, somebody that tries their best but doesn't get what they want."

"A moral dilemma one feels with a character who is both good and bad. Delivering this cognitive dissonance to an unexpected and faithful audience who would leave the film feeling conflicted at themselves for feeling sympathetic for a villain", she said.

We created a character that was both recognisable but unique. Like us they had demanding desires, they had a pedestal through selfish means but as they looked at the world they stood on, their pedestal began to crumble at the feet of forsaken children, buried by the bruises and blood of violence.

The Basi no longer mattered. This huge beacon of success had blinded the character and so many others from the harsh reality of neglect. There was nothing else to aim for, nothing else left to prove. This woman had seen her face in the sky countless times, simply by looking up and seeing the sun and the stars and she was tired of the view.

I threaded Will's words with my own to create a riveting plot full of showstopping speeches and moving metaphors.

The film would end with a black screen, allowing the audience to see themselves staring back at a title card.

'You can build your own Basi within you, if you just help others to do the same. 'Save the children and save yourself.'

Florence called Will and told him to meet us at a bar.

He was already there by the time we arrived carrying our manuscripts and pitches.

"So you took my script and made it into a story, you used your connections to create a vision for change?"

"When you think of a villain you think of people they have hurt, never why they became the villain, they are bad and that is their whole selves summed up in a single word. But they are actually just someone that needs saving, it is not just our children we have been abandoning."

"John told me about Mark so we created a character and placed a true spotlight upon their life and if you still believe they are bad after that then at least you have given them a fair shot and isn't a fair shot all any of us need?", said Florence.

"With everything we knew we made this, something the public will consume, by amplifying your World and the Faceless will fall. We want change, we want meaning, we think this is the first step to getting there. We are dismantling the Faceless and putting humans back in their rightful place, a pedestal of production, giving them the right to feel alive again." I spoke.

The film showed the children, the mass mountains of dead bodies, bloodied at the Faceless' hands. The only clear villain was the idleness that the Faceless had tethered us with.

Slowly the impacts of the film became clear, people were forsaking their Faceless and turning to Will for reason.

Chapter Thirty Eight

Florence

My final role was one of my own creation, conceived with the aim of inciting change, empowering watchers to take back their lives.

My character was inspiring, she held a candle to me that said it was okay. I could be forgiven for the errors staining my past and would once again find the light in my future.

I flicked through the photo flashes in my mind and recalled all the days I had attended award shows, holding shiny metal structures in my hand at the end of the night, smiling as I delivered my rehearsed scripts.

Now I had no rehearsed lines, I was my authentic self. I no longer had a Faceless thing telling me what to say to keep people wanting me.

The film's success came in its lack of adoration, there were no Faceless ceremonies as many of the watchers had forsaken them, realising it was time for them to try something different, to think of others. I had been a figurehead to this revolution and I finally felt whole.

I set about practising Will's teachings, I destroyed my passion plaque and headed into the city to try and save more children.

They barely had enough skin left clutching their bones, their eyes bulging and frightful as I approached. I didn't believe in ghosts but their visible bones and gaunt expression convinced me that you do not have to be dead to haunt.

I had always known they were there but I had never wanted to see them, never wanted to look and now I stared.

This is what Will had meant when he said I had filled my life with things to hide the holes.

So many of these skeletal creatures crawled the walls, trying to take up as little room as possible, whilst the others, slightly bigger, watched me wildly, their tongues mimicking the tempo of my footsteps.

I produced my Famia slowly and felt their blades on me. I wiped the glass cartridge onto my tongue and placed it at my feet as food appeared, I took a few steps back and gestured to them to take the food.

They leapt on it with the same ferocity that cameras had once done when they flashed at me as I stood on the red carpet.

"I have more, I can take some of you to a place where there is more, there is warmth."

They looked at me blankly so I rubbed my stomach and my shoulders. A few of the older ones nodded, keeping their blades close but not brandished as they followed.

I took them to Will's estate. It was larger than 50 of the penthouses threaded together.

There were people timidly tending to vegetable gardens and others slowly following instructions in the kitchen. There were a few children being read to patiently by an older child who was confidently reading passage ways under the supervision of a young adult.

I found Will in a room full of books. I still had the children surrounding me as I smiled at him for support. He took them from me, calling for one of the helpers who came with blankets and food.

"You've got quite the community connecting together."

He nodded. "There is still so much that needs to be done." He gestured around the room, observing each old book spine before speaking again, "I want this for the children but larger, a library, I need buildings to begin again."

"Well, you'll need a builder then", I said.

Chapter Thirty Nine

Mark

The angry man broke out of me, his blood boiling as he burned through my skin when I woke that morning. I had been asleep for several days, my body broken by my own beating.

The angry man sat beside me and I came to know his name was once love. We wept together as he taught me who he once was and what he had sadly become.

He held my broken knuckles to my eyes as he told me who we had hurt, he kissed my head as he poked the dent in it. He held my hand as he cried, his bloodshot eyes so sore I thought at first they were bleeding. He told me how we were so fortunate to be alive, so fortunate to bear this pain, to have these bruises when those who had given them to us had died.

Why was I still in this body? Why was I sentenced to this skeleton? I screamed so violently that I startled the angry man. I begged him to leave me and he told me I was not ready yet, my wounds still sore, my heart still heavy. He said he would wait by my side until he knew I could do it alone.

Here I was again under the same bush, under the same weight, in the same park full of different drinks and drugs but devoid of dreams.

I had no desire but the desire to have nothing anymore, to stop this feeling, to go back to my bricks, to a woman I once knew. To go back there, to Jill, that is what I wanted but I knew that my life with her was all buried under here with me in this bush. My legs stained with bird excrement, my head heavy with the weight of what I had done, and the emptiness of who I would now never be.

I looked at the angry man and begged him for his help, if he could help me stop the drugs, stop the drink, he could help me be okay, he could help me stand-alone again. He smiled meekly, this was the first step.

I had to quit but I knew I would struggle in my survival. This was too easy for me to access, easier than the things I loved, easier than building. I could inhale happiness, I could inject love. It was so beautiful and brutal and it was going to end my life.

I will not let this bush or the bar be my final burial place. I will build houses on the land I once almost died on.

I stumble upwards and head for a blurry bench, pulling a damaged Famia out of my pocket, relieved to see it still had two capsules left in it, I spit on it and it brings me water. A passer-by shakes their head at me whilst another, a face I recognise from the bar, turns and runs in the opposite direction.

A man in a suit briefly stopped and told me I didn't look well, he offered me a pill he said would help me. I told him I couldn't but he promised it would make me feel better, gesturing toward my wounds so I took it, barely looking into his eyes.

It began to rain and as the water hit my skin I started to laugh. I could feel the air in my brain like it had stormed for 50 days and now the world was still. I could feel a woman with me, her thin blonde hair blowing in my face. She was young, she was firm, her narrow fingers interlaced with mine, she was smiling but cautious, and she was close to me.

I braided her hair in our house as she sobbed about the Voice, I kissed her neck and promised I would make it all alright. I remember her in a white dress, small blue flowers in her hair. I remember her happiness and I laugh as tears run down my nose.

I screamed as I saw myself shout at her, frightened of my own insecurities and the trap they had set out for me. I screamed at myself as I lied to her, convincing her I had produced something to be proud of while drowning in drink. I broke down as I saw myself smashing a bird house I had built for her.

She was still in that house. I wanted to go back to her but I knew I never could, she wouldn't take me back, she wasn't the same woman and I wasn't worthy of her touch anymore. I had become the voice in her head, I had to let her rest, I had to let her go.

I remember bricks in my palm, red, yellow, brown, and grey dust on my fingertips and on my arms, like little freckles of the future splattered on my skin. Something I was part of, something I was making, a creation.

A man of purpose, a man of substance. Then the darkness descended and I was drinking again. All my masterpieces dissolved like the little pills I sipped at.

A man appeared in my vision. I was no longer in my memories.

"What?", I snapped.

"Hi Mark."

I swallowed, "Yep, what do you want?"

"How was the pill?"

"What pill?"

"You just took a pill before we spoke, you sat there in silence for ten minutes with a look of loss on your face, I am assuming that was the pill. Can you tell me who you are, Mark?"

"I'm a drinker, I'm a laugh, I'm a loud one, I am whatever you want me to be. Who are you?"

"I'm Will and you're right, you are a drinker, you're a killer too. I know that you think that is okay to do but how did it make you feel Mark?"

"Look mate, I don't know you and I don't know how you know me, but I am done, I am done with it now."

"Are you really done, Mark? If I walked away and never stopped to see you again, would you be able to promise that I could do so knowing you wouldn't go back to those bars? Knowing you wouldn't end someone's life again?"

The angry man switched his light on. I tried to swallow him down but he stood staring, his hand on the sheath.

"You can tell me who you are Mark, can you still tell me who you want to be?"

I looked at him. I couldn't figure out what his deal was but I told him what the pill had shown me, surprised by how smooth the truth slipped off my tongue.

"A broken man crushed by the weight of his own potential, the pressure to be this perfect man, loving husband, dutiful builder with a purpose and pride in his creation. I like that man, I could agree with him, even respect him. But this man in front of me is not yet that man, he once was but now no longer. I can help with that Mark, I can bring you back to who you once were."

He paused, watching me for a reaction. The pill had left a chalky texture on the roof of my mouth that lulled me into a silence, buttressed by the bollards of booze still flooding my mind.

Booze was an attractive woman with sun-kissed hair and big eyes, drugs were her voluptuous best friend, both of them were waving, their long fingers beckoning to me.

Will pierced through this image with his domineering voice.

"I have a project not too dissimilar to the ones you used to produce. I know that is upsetting for you now, all your efforts erased by Faceless who disregard your vision. Your project takes too long in their eyes so they let you play whilst they build a 'better' version of your building. My project would let you build your buildings, providing they are up to the standard they once were. I want you to be him again, think about it, don't drink on it, and call me."

The women in their short skirts and low-cut tops returned, their fingers no longer beckoning, their lips no longer smiling. They were angry and impatient, their faces disgruntled and greying. I wanted to watch them but knew I had to walk away.

Chapter 40

Henry

Jill stopped speaking for a while after the fight with Mark. After I had told her that it had been him who had ended the lives of my friends, of children.

She still sat in her usual spot most mornings, counting the birds, but she didn't watch TV, she watched the back of her eyelids and entered other worlds.

It took months for my bruises to heal but once they had done, I was stronger, I was no longer scared. I had injured the mountain man, I had watched him writhe around his own skeleton. He was angrier than me and wounded. I no longer feared but pitied him.

With Jill resting, I left the sleeping section. I was straight into a shop, buying famia capsules with the points I had accumulated from hitting Mark's eye and shin.

Everything else in the shop was dull, uninteresting, and unappealing, until my eyes landed on a guitar. It was intricately carved and the perfect size for me.

I returned to Jill with it, presenting her with the fully stocked famia and showing her what I understood.

Gently, I stroked the strings and made the sounds of the birds we had watched together. She watched me from the bed with tears in her eyes.

I practised like this for days, watching the man on the screen like I had done once before. Finding my fingers, finding my form, and figuring myself out as I played.

Jill started to stay down with me for longer, listening to me play. One day she brought down a camera with her. It had a few scuff marks and a couple of the buttons were broken but I could record myself playing quite well. I would share these videos with the world.

This is how our days went, she would sing to the birds, sing to my songs and I would play them for her, both of us in harmony after the war.

Chapter Forty One

Mark

I sat on that bench for a while, as the rain cleared and the sun kissed the trees again, I felt my bones begin to dry. I brushed my hands along the warm metal of its structure, noticing the plaque on the centre that read, 'sit back and feed the birds that fly so freely', and I realised where I was.

I had first met Jill on this bench, I imagined the fabric fibres caught in the bolts to be part of her scarf and swallowed a little sob.

To indulge with self-loathing would only send me back to the bar.

I had nowhere to be, I had places I wanted to crawl to but knew that my want to get better would defeat my want to wilt. After a day or so of aimless walking and biting cold evenings, I found a phone box and called Will.

I told him I was ready to get better and he knew in time that this would be true.

He found me, stretched out his arm, and took me to his estate. Far out from the penthouses, away from the city.

I remember the shock of no Faceless helping Will to maintain such a household. Later I would learn a new word, 'helpers'. He had real human beings that supported him in exchange for housing.

One of which tended to me. She called herself a doctor, explaining she understood what was best for my recovery.

Will had found her on the side of the street close to death when she was younger than 10, he had brought her here and looked after her. She repaid him by reading all she could about medical remedies in old books, in rooms full of books which he referred to as libraries.

As I sweated out the drugs and screamed for more when they had left my system, she would be standing there in the corner of my blurred vision.

She would calm me as I envisioned death and devoured its. I saw the birth of darkness and danger as I sweated into the abyss, she was there for me in and out of it all. She was reminding me why I was here, telling me this is what I had chosen, this is what I had wanted and to go through the beast is to destroy it.

Through the fever and the ice, I didn't think I could still be alive but there was my hand and hers on my chest, up and down and up and down, like boats in ocean I had never stood on the shore of, the world inside my stomach, societies of ruin spilt onto my chest.

I could not sleep, I could not be awake, I could only feel the darkness. I starved my skeleton to rid myself from all that I had indulged in.

The fear of the famia producing more alcohol, the fantasy these visions provided me kept my fingers crawling toward the door as my mind fragmented to keep itself together.

I had to be isolated, I was given sleep in the form of thick air, that kept me still and silent for days to stop the screaming. My famia was taken off me and I was provided with fresh food from Will's kitchen.

I still wasn't completely correct many months later with my body breaking out into tremors or sweats at any given moment. I couldn't look into the face of alcohol without sensing its smile and wanting eyes.

As I gained strength I would leave my bed, slowly and cautiously I started to wander the vast corridors of Will's world. He had an extensive collection of rooms, all serving a unique purpose.

I walked around and admired its structure. Neo-Renaissance, baroque and bold in its beauty, each corner carved to hold the sky of the room.

Sometimes, when the sun was shining, I ventured outside. I could never cover the full ground, especially in my state but I managed to walk around the main house, beguiled by its beauty.

It was intricate and bold without being intimidating, each second and third floor window had a balcony and two of the outer walls boasted tall turrets. Its brick was golden and red, a house that looked like a city but felt like a home.

The sense of strong symmetry and intricate detail evoked harmony and synergy, each external feature infused with connection to create a unified front.

One day Will caught me in one of his many libraries and said, "All a person needs in this life Mark, is a good book and good food and someone to share it with. Only through learning will we gain the courage to be curious and only this curiosity can lead to change."

I nodded, feeling myself tremble a little.

"Your progress has been proficient Mark, how do you feel?"

I want to say free as I finally feel lighter but there are still two firm hands on both my shoulders preventing me from taking the leap and they belong to shame and guilt.

"I am getting there", I mumbled.

"Productivity will cure you, I think a few more weeks of physical recovery where you will sleep, you will be sick and you will gorge on the finest words our greatest minds have to offer and then you will be ready."

Through the sickness and the relentless sweats, through the darkness, to find my hand rubbing my chest, I learned to face the shame, I learned its name: Mark and the man he had let down.

I wondered why he had arrived and taken the place of the person who once stood before him, the person who loved his wife. The man who had wanted to remind her of her strength, to show her the world again, the man who wanted to create buildings not break them all down. I saw the sickness and called it healing.

8 suns later Will entered my chambers and called me better, passing me some old blue overalls. Someone had embroidered my name onto the chest in white cursive. I

smiled, it had been a while since I had associated it with pride.

Will told me I had healed because I wanted to and now it was time to reclaim who I was meant to be. Outside, he led me to a bird bath that had been broken when it had been hit by a tree from a recent storm, the branches dislodging the stone head so it lay miserable beside its plinth rather than proudly on top of it.

"Your skills are needed here Mark, not in the bar, not on the streets, they are needed here to repair this bird bath. If I leave you with the necessary tools for a few hours can I put my faith in you to have it completed by the time I am back?"

With tears in my eyes I nodded, he walked away and I knelt by the plinth, the miserable square with the chip on its side, lay weeping as I sobbed with pride. It had been years since I had built anything and this time I would be doing it knowing it was needed, not as a distraction but as a duty.

I got it done in an hour and went to find Will.

This journey was how I spent my days, rising with Will and eating with the helpers in the kitchen, enjoying proper cooked meals made using fresh ingredients in the garden and animals on the farm.

I had not had food from a famia for many months but I remembered the rubbery texture it provided compared to the richness of this in front of me.

The rest of the day, until almost dark, would be spent on completing tasks. There was a wall in the allotment that had come loose, a bench that needed to be built for the garden and a room that needed to be divided in two for more children. Each day I would complete the task before the time set and then I would go and search for more.

I lost track of how many days were spent this way but one that changed the course of the rest happened after I had just built a bridge over the stream in the garden.

As usual, I finished my production earlier than planned so entered the house, removing the mud from my shoes and shaking down my clothes before proceeding.

I asked around for Will to the helpers who were busy attending to their own duties. Rosie, one of the gardeners, was collecting water for her saplings and Oscar, one of the many chefs, was chopping onions preparing for tonight's dinner. They didn't bother themselves with what Will would be doing but suggested he would be in one of the libraries in the east wing.

And there he was, wearing the sun, he sat, slumped in a peacock chair, chewing a pen and frowning at his paper. He saw me and smiled.

"The bridge is built, took me a little longer than I thought."

"Why's that Mark?"

I often wondered if each word Will uttered was a test, I was never sure what to say to him.

Puzzled, I muttered, "Well it's just me."

"It is just you Mark and although you are quite skilled, you are intricate and hardworking, it is just you. You have met Oscar, Rosie, Harriet, Charlie, Beth, Florence and John, you know some of them are on the same team from the kitchen, to the garden, to the maintenance of this house, whereas you are the only builder."

I let this word linger for a while, letting it forge itself onto my brain, no longer a killer or an addict but a builder. I was back where I was meant to be, a small smile stretched into my skin.

I nodded. He was silent as he wrote something else down, smiling to himself as he pushed a stop into the paper.

"Where do you think my helpers came from Mark?"

"I know they aren't Faceless but I don't know where they are from."

"They were people just like you, unsupported, undervalued, neglected by the norms of society, many of whom were driven to drink, driven to drugs to escape their meaningless reality. I gave them purpose and pride by bringing them here. Do you not think this is better?"

"This is better, this is what we should be doing. If there are more people that need to be saved from themselves then I'm the one that can find them."

Will got up from his seat and passed me his paper,

"This is my manuscript. Florence and John made this into a film, it influenced many and they are coming, they are coming here to find sanctuary. Your workload is about to increase and I need you to find a team to build spaces for these people, for the children. I need you to create the future I have promised."

I read a few pages of the manuscript, realising I was wasting my time, I knew the state of the world because I had played a part in its demise. There were people out there who needed me as much as I needed them. I could use my skills to save them, I could silence the angry man by turning blood into bandages and save the suffering.

Chapter Forty Two

Jada

I hadn't noticed the fall of the Faceless. Of course, I had heard of the film but I had been too busy writing my songs and spending hours in my home built studio recording my music.

I knew what I wanted to do so I just kept doing it. My shows were still selling and when I heard nothing from my Faceless about gigs booked and tickets sold I just looked into doing it myself.

I did feel disheartened when I no longer saw myself on the Basi, accepting that maybe someone else was about to take my spot, but I told myself that was fine if they were better than me then so be it; I was still enjoying myself so I didn't let it stop my performances.

It was the faces a few of my friends had begun to wear that reminded me something was wrong.

"Only 10 people came to my opera last night and the week before that it peaked at 15. My passion plaque and Faceless are both unresponsive", said Anya sipping on apple seltzer, she had ordered champagne.

"Same with mine! For weeks now I have been trying to get this new track out, but there have been no takers", said MILK.

"My passion plaque doesn't respond, my famia brings no fruition and my Faceless is silent. I haven't eaten in two days", Ali complained.

I asked Benny to make my friends some food and he did so graciously. Between bites, I watched my friend's perplexed faces. They were angry, they were confused but they were not questioning why this was happening. They believed that if they were unhappy, because they were special enough, some divine force would hear their wants and help.

You are your own divine force.

I kept quiet about not feeling the impacts and instead asked, "You guys have any idea why it might be happening? Mine has been pretty silent too."

"Well, you saw that film right? The face of the world?", said MILK.

I stared blankly at him.

"Okay, Jada, how have you not seen it? Well the people that made this film are part of a group who go around collecting the nobodies, the desperate and the desolate and taking them off to some place. Apparently, they're doing this thing called work."

"What does that mean?", I asked.

"So you know we spend our time pursuing what we want and always getting it? Well, for those people that fell off the more conventional path this group is making them productive, turning their passions into progressions", MILK explained.

"But my Faceless was doing that.", said Anya.

"Exactly, you aren't. Do you ever think that you're not the talented one? The Faceless is and it has just granted you your fortune because you wanted it, you didn't actually earn it?", said MILK.

I silently observed this interaction, realising that for the first time since I was in my early teens, I was self-sufficient, I had no Faceless paving the way for me, I had been doing it myself. I had no need for others to tell me I was good.

"So you know this group?"

"I know of the group and all of them seem a lot happier, they say they put in the hours pursuing what they love, producing an outlet that connects them to the people around them and they're full of pride rather than expectancy", said MILK.

"Yeah you know what reckon I could do it on my own", said Ali.

"Well I know I can do it on my own. I would just prefer it if my Faceless did it. I know I want to act, but I don't know if I can without it so if this group can allow me to do that then I will", said Anya.

"Jada, are you joining the boycott and finding this group?"

"My Faceless went silent a couple of months ago and I got rid of my passion plaque", I confessed.

Their faces paled with disbelief, a sheet of shock stared back at me in the place of their once admiring smiles.

"Honestly, I just started doing it myself and people kept coming to the gigs but MILK, Ali you are talented and Anya, I don't know why only 10 people came to your opera, your voice would sell out shows Faceless or not", I continued.

"So you're not coming to find this group?"

"No, I am happy being the person that creates a crowd I don't want to be someone that becomes one but thank you."

They left the bar. I haven't seen or heard from them since. The group aren't nomadic, they still live in houses but we are divided, I live in a world that they were not sieved into, meaning their talent was never true.

I believe they are happy now, or at least that is how I imagine them, they must be smiling to continue pushing the boulder up the hill.

Despite the world changing, my stages shifting, and spotlights flickering, I still stood at the top, settled into the view. Singing was what I had been born to do.

I was still the phoenix my Nani had told me to be, this absence of known faces was just another pile of ashes I had to dust myself from. Benny had stayed loyal to me, I was not alone. I thought of John and which world he may have gone to.

For a moment I let myself miss him, I let myself mourn, I was at the funeral of my friendships, at a future I could have explored. I was being dragged off my stage by the forces that had built it for me, the spotlight shut off and left to sing in the dark.

Then I dusted my feathers off and remembered who I was. My voice was all that I truly had and if I could no longer use it I may as well be dead and I didn't deserve that yet. I already understood what success was, I felt it whenever I sang, I saw it on the faces in the crowd.

Sitting again in the detox bar, the Faceless malfunctioning and serving the incorrect orders, I thought back to the first time I met John, the hope we had for each other, for ourselves. All the time we had taken to carve ourselves into the people we knew we needed to be.

Sat at the back sipping a drink I had not ordered or wanted, he found me, with an excited expression etched into his essence. As he sat opposite me and I fell into the features of his face once more I knew he no longer wore the face of that man I could have once loved.

His head was directed differently, his thoughts corrupted and cruel. His bitter resentment had led him to threaten the livelihoods of all those he had once wanted to be a part of.

He felt he had been exiled from his hometown so he had tried to build another, the foundations built on the basis of somebody else's guidance. He would never understand that in order to live your own life you must build your own home, if not you will always be living on the side streets in someone else's life.

I had to try and be happy for him. After all, he had finally done it, he had used his writing to create change, but they were not his words, he was a fraud through and through. I stared at him as he spoke, my eyes glistening with sentimental melancholy and pity.

"You saw the film right? You have conquered this world, why not be part of another, one where you can influence others?", he said, almost pleading.

"John, I am a singer, I inspire, I excite, I am a party after a dark night. I am not struggling, I am not desperate. Have you ever seen me on my knees, pleading for saviour, for drugs, drink, or any other debauchery desire I may demand? A happy person understands that anything external will not direct the weather of your mood, it is all within. I never relied on a Faceless, I only ever saw myself. I am staying here, this is my world and it is enough for me."

"Jada the world will change, I just want you to be a part of the process, I want you to be a part of my world."

"The only world I need to be a part of is my own", I said as he turned to his shoes.

He lingered, our silence a farewell. I knew he would prosper as would I but we would both have to do so without one another.

He nodded, stood up and without turning around, he left.

I still sing on stages just to much fewer faces, my songs still felt by those who go unseen.

Benny stayed by my side, listening to my songs, and providing me with the food that I desired and the company I needed. I know I am one of the lucky ones who has enough power to put the will into the want and find my way.

You have to be good enough to break the mould, but people never tell you the mould you fit is different to the one they want to pour you in to.

Chapter Forty Three

Will

People appeared at the edges of my estate, evaporating from their previous existence and into a new one. Some credited the film as saving them, whilst others had found my manuscript.

But I could still feel the pull of others that needed just a little more push into persuasion, luring me to the city. With John, Florence, and occasionally Mark, we returned to the streets.

After the children had been saved we moved on to the haunted, those with a perpetual look of shock on their faces but sedation behind their eyes. I appeared as a double and became an army in the eyes of a drunkard.

We didn't want them to fear us but they did at first, to blockade themselves from saviour, to keep themselves small. There were a few that approached us timidly at first then desperate as we turned to leave, pleading with us to take them too. We told them if they could persuade their friends to join we would take them.

Then there were the quiet ones, the ones that claimed it was just one drink, that it had been their own fault they hadn't wanted it enough so of course they had been unsuccessful, one drink would remedy this disappointment and it would get better tomorrow. I told them they didn't have any tomorrows left but if they defied their Faceless they could have a future, and they could drive their own dreams.

These types were more reluctant, staring out at something no one else could see, not particularly enjoying the contents of their drink but sipping anyway, unaware of what they wanted other than to be a part of something.

"No one here knows your name, I know a place where everyone knows everyone and I can see you fitting in there", I would preached.

After a few meetings they acquiesced, nodding slowly as they sat their glass down, handing me their passion plaque and leaving.

Bar by bar we recruited the majority, destroying the Faceless before shutting the door. Then there were the bars we could not enter for they frequented those too far gone to save, the drunken dead.

Back at my estate, after months of rest and self-torture, after remedies and dark recoveries, I gathered the new faces.

"When you are exhausted, when there is sweat on your forehead and air in your lungs, you are your most alive, this is the only form of success and it is one that will make you smile. Save yourself from weak promises, pursue productivity and you will change the world. To work is to be successful. With the world we are working to create you will be able to trade your exercises in for tangible resources, for physical accolades that will achieve an emotional goal."

A few apprehensive applauds and faces still recovering from an internal war answered, then the sounds of the souls I had saved echoed out from their stations of duty, cheering furiously. And suddenly the unsettled strangers become one voice full of hope.

Stood at my pedestal before them all, I smiled, this was the sound of success.

Chapter Forty Four

Mark

Everything starts slowly, existing imperceptibly. It is intricate and deliberate, you start a moment with its lasting memory propelling it forward. I was out in the heat again, the sun smiling down on me as I sweated happily into the bricks and mortar that were moulding me.

Using old blueprints produced by a Faceless, I was to build a Discite. It was an ambitious project, one that required 10 hours of labour each day.

I wasn't just myself anymore, there were many more of me all working in unity. They too had had the screaming nights and sleepless days but like me, they were doing better. If we stopped working it would be for water brought to us fresh from the kitchen, or to share a joke or a story about how we had survived ourselves.

I powered through the headaches but the dizziness slowed me down, using the stories and water breaks as an excuse to sit. Not wanting to let my team down I forced myself to continue to lift. This eventually led me to be sick and I was escorted back into the house for bed rest.

Sickness had never been something I had experienced before drinking, I had never wanted to feel the consequence of my own indulgences but when the need for alcohol took away from my wants it had more power over me than I of it.

Its grasp was still inside of me, trying to unstitch the threads I had managed to pull myself together with but I would be stronger this time. My seams reinforced by the smiling faces surrounding me, and the crumbs of brick once again on my palms.

Through the blurred vision and fumbling fizz in my chest, I dreamt of Jill. I apologised to her through my hazes, hoping she would somehow hear. I had learned that I would not be forgiven and this was not a reason to be angry, this was the price of keeping the angry man quiet.

She wasn't the same in my mind as when she first stepped through the corridors of my cranium. She walked boldly now, only staying with my dusty thoughts fleetingly, leaving me feeling as though I had dragged her away from something more important.

Her hair was fuller and her eyes had a knowing gleam to them, she didn't want to waste her time with me anymore, she was telling me to let her go. But like the bottle, her scent lingered and I longed for her.

The intermittency of my failings was a constant battle, fighting for restoration and redemption whilst my body battled with the weight of itself. It took another 6 weeks before I returned to the projects, only to find that the team had expanded to 25 and the first building was almost complete.

A hiss of resentment filled my stomach before I pushed it down, proud of the people who were producing what I was unable to do and happy I could now assist.

Will had returned from his recruiting, it had been successful, there were several screams coming from various rooms as I entered his quarters.

"Mark, the Discite is coming on well, the first building is finished and I can see the second building has made solid progress. You have worked hard. How are you feeling?"

My eyes were always sore and my limbs were always angry at me for making them move but my soul felt as though it was breathing again.

"Can't complain."

He put a bottle of Bourbon on the table and unscrewed the lid.

"Perhaps a reward?", he gestured, lifting the bottle toward me.

An old friend, waving at me, running to embrace me after too long. A beloved memory. The warm fuzz and the easy laughing, the sweet burn of harmony among strangers. Then the blackness and the fog within it, the distant calls and eerie echoes, the blood on my knuckles and the guilt in my gut.

He thought he was testing me, he was tormenting me, taunting me with the sweetest temptation, knowing that this feeling of peace was all that I wanted but understanding that if I sipped it, I would finish the bottle and with it, everything I had produced would crumble.

"Why would you even suggest that?", I spat.

He nodded and apologised, smiling to himself as he put it back into a locked cabinet.

"Why did you refuse it? I would not have imposed any ramifications onto you", he asked.

"Because I would be unable to do what I wanted if I gave into the demands of my desires. These demons are trying to prevent me from being the person I know I am becoming."

He nodded.

"Will, I am trying to do better, I want to do better, I want to build the world you speak of, I want to live long. Perhaps one day I shall have children and they will learn how to be better in the Disicte their father helped to build."

10 months later, I hadn't sniffed a drink, had not itched for drugs. I had pleaded for production. Through my tremors, through my dizziness, through my fatigue I always found myself aching for the sweet kiss of the sun and the smiles of my mates as we built.

We finished the entire Discite. It had separate rooms, Will referred to as classrooms, several staircases, and a grand hall. It had an outhouse for drama and a gymnasium. It was 2 stories tall and full of grandeur.

An institution that exuded power and positivity, a place of progression, red and orange brick, warm and familiar, a fresh stretch of the field for exploration and exercise. A slide and roundabout, a swing set and seesaw, all words I had only seen on the pages of the books that Will showed me.

He showed us how they should work and applauded us when we succeeded, allowing us to use our creation. Sat on the swing I felt a distant nostalgia rising within me as the world fell away from my feet.

This gentle rocking motion was so alien yet familiar to me, the humm of a gentle mother and the soft watch of a loving father fell onto me. Then as I got higher and faster my heart echoing the pace, a burst of adrenaline shot through me.

Triumphant and ridiculous I couldn't help but laugh. It was the same reaction for most of the team who had to lightly wrestle each other off.

This was the feeling we would create for our children, for the next generation. This feeling was better than any drink or any drug I had injected or made myself sick from, they echoed each other in their might but the feeling of the swing set within me was so organic. I was happy to be sharing it with the future.

Chapter Forty Five

Jill

The birds were shrill that cool winter morning, the sleeping section still quiet and emptier than before. I made my usual coffee and sat by the window, the plumage of the birds so vibrant my cup went cold from staring outside for too long. Henry would be playing in two hours. There was nothing on TV.

Upstairs, I opened the wardrobe, its bare bones glared at me. My vest tops and sweats, my one summer dress, all greying from neglect. Mark's clothes still stood bold as though his body filled them.

It had been a few years since our fight, although I often relived that night just to remember it differently, oh how things could have been. I do not stay in these fictionalised scenes for too long, it is unsafe for me to see him as the man he could have been, I had to think of him as the man he was.

But still, I took his coat and held it close. It had frayed at the edges, its seams on the shoulders beginning to sag. It no longer smelled of him, it just felt cold. But I loved its distressed details and tired shape, it was proof that Mark, how I had once known him, had existed for me. Putting it on I looked outside. I wasn't trembling as much as I once had done.

Each step down was a mountain conquered and then at the door, I waited. No one was coming to open it for me, no one was coming to push me out, there was no dark voice on the other side telling me what I had not done. There was just me and the edge of opportunity.

Henry had been playing guitar for hundreds for a while now, he had always asked me to come out and see him and I hadn't ever felt able to. I hadn't counted the birds this morning, I had simply enjoyed their existence. Change was happening and it was about time I joined it.

I opened the door and stepped out.

There were no internal earthquakes, no crack at each step. Timid at first, an eternity passed as I walked down my front garden, breathing in the sweet air. I stood still. Nothing was happening. I was alone within myself and I couldn't help but smile.

I started running, taking stolen years back, my pace fastened and my heart drummed, my body my own marching band cheering me on. My breath drowning my lungs, as I choked happily for air. I screamed with pride, with rage. I felt possible. I felt brave.

Leaving the sleeping section I was instantly at Henry's gig. The crowd was already busy but I stumbled in with strangers, all here to see my son.

Not only a talented musician but the boy I had so often cradled, cared for, and cried with. All his hopes his own, his dreams delivered, he stood on stage to admiring fans cheering his name, and then his eyes met mine and he started to cry as he played on. I could hear the music but I stood in silence as I watched the boy I loved become the man he was meant to be.

And then something washed over me. Rain. Mark had gone, I had to accept it, if he were not dead, he was not here and here was where I wanted him to be. Henry no longer needed me and I didn't want to return home again. It had become a graveyard where all I had once wanted and had, was now no longer. A bird fell from the sky into a puff of feathers at my feet, dead, its blue and yellow plumage turning as dark as a wet stone.

With the songs playing on I left and found myself facing the ocean.

She was cold and large but her strength was settling, soothed by her presence, I wrapped Mark's coat tighter around me. I stood alone, that was okay, this single shadow had been my constant companion for many years. This solace was what I needed.

I had done all I wanted, I had watched the birds, I had watched my shows, I had loved so deeply and generously I was swollen with it, I saw my son play. I had lived a good and full life.

Filling my pockets with rocks and looking up to the sky one last time to see a dove flying above me. I smiled as I walked into the sea and let the waves swallow me.

Chapter Forty Six

Henry

My grief for Jill, who I had come to know as mum, became my best selling commodity before the fall of the Faceless. The odes I wrote to her, the spotlight I had shone in the crowd where she had once stood was a constant testament to the light she had been for me.

To suffer was my legacy, heartbreak became my happy place as it drenched my soul in more music which led to more applause and accolades. Once burdened with anger and consuming regret, transformed into a legacy of resilience and artistry, to suffer was to be successful.

I toured for a while, finding children on the streets and providing them with food, water, shelter and music lessons with all of my passion points. I chased change and found it when I met Will.

I brought him out on stage with all the children he had helped save on the final show of my final tour. Most of them were into their early adulthood now and having a wealth of knowledge they sang in harmony or played their instruments to the final three songs of my set, all the crowd speechless for sobs.

At the end of the show, I shook his hand and helped to teach street children survival through song and to prevent others from ending up this way.

Chapter Forty Seven

John

The Faceless had begun to malfunction with fewer people wanting their services, their resources made redundant and their structure collapsing. Soon wanting something wouldn't be enough anymore, Will's world was winning.

We had saved so many of the next generation, with many choosing to save themselves. Not wanting to forsake a face I still tried most weekends to save many more.

Will had destroyed my famia and provided me with what he called real food from his gardens, it tasted like it had a story so I accepted it.

I tried to share it with the children, some feebly took it whilst others wept for more, which the kitchen was always happy to provide. As they chewed I would read to them. I read them the manuscript and showed them our film.

With the Discite built and homes opened, I had started writing once more, but it was no longer the words that filled me, it was the faces I shared them with.

Slowly I taught the children which words corresponded with which misconnection they were feeling. I taught them to hold a pen and write what they were feeling. Despite the perpetual shelter and abundance of food that now filled them most of them wrote empty, or alone or cold. They were echoes of children, our desires had destroyed a once invincible generation.

In between meals and communication lessons they were told to play on the sets that Mark and his team had built but they did not know how. Except for the occasional ball toss between the older children, their childhood setting was silence.

I wrote a story about childhood play and read it to them whilst sitting on a spinning roundabout. It was a story about safety and how they could now smile without fear again.

There were a few nods and some of the younger children started using the slide although scared too at first, they finally started smiling. I brought in a poem about rejection and explained how like them I had felt rejected too. I had worked hard to pursue my passion and it had once been what the people wanted. In time they learned to love other things and my words got left behind.

I told them in the previous world my efforts were overlooked, and the demands of my desires had left me desolate. But now I could share them and finally, I was being heard and recognised for my word. I told them they had once been invisible when they had always deserved to be seen, and everyone looked to them now, full of love and full of care.

Will gives me what he calls the 'classics', to teach them about heartbreak and broken families. The older children fell quiet when I read these, looking to their shoes for support whilst the younger ones asked what family meant.

"To have a family is to feel secure, to feel loved and listened to, if someone is your family they look out for you", I explained.

After this some of them started calling me family.

In time there was trust and the younger ones learned quickly that they could trust the shelter they were under and chose to sleep inside instead of on the harsh cobbles. Soon they were writing wobbly sentences about sunsets on sleepless streets and golden cities where they were loved.

When we could, Will and I would go back out to the streets to find other lost children and were happy that each time we went, we found less and less. As the Faceless started to crumble, people had to focus on what they had not yet achieved, many of them turned to Will to demonstrate they could save themselves by contributing to a world that would save everybody else.

Sometimes Will would play music. It was always quiet but always moving and evoked memories of Jada.

You can want to be good at something, you can even tell yourself you're good at it but this will never be the case until your strengths are needed by somebody else and now mine are. But there will always be a need for music, there always has been and Jada would be good, Faceless or not.

My original ambitions may be left unfulfilled, a fading memory of fame and stardom, a world I used to call success but the dust on my shelves and the creases in the corners seem further away from me now. On my days of space, there is always the possibility to unfurl those pages and try again but I cannot bring myself to start, too focused on the young minds I have to inspire.

I had always struggled to create fictional worlds, left doubting my true ability to mould them. Now sitting at the head of the Discite classroom, I knew that perhaps I hadn't been able to change my own world, but I could change the world of others.

Chapter Forty Eight

Florence

Will was right, everyone here was celebrated for being themselves as long as they shared with others. Those who had previously been shunned to their sleeping sections to pursue their passions could do so openly here. The sewists who became clothing designers or the growers, once sentenced to their small slice of grass, now tended to the vast gardens.

I enjoyed the schedule of things, rising with the sun, I learned to appreciate its beauty instead of berating its existence. I would teach until late, working through the imaginations of the future to direct them to their best path before marking up their ideas and going to the communal dinner.

Outside Will's estate, construction was well underway, soon we would have more houses. At this point, we had a cinema, a library and the Discite.

There were rumours that restaurants would be opening up but I enjoyed the community of the grand hall, eating with strangers who were becoming family, finding faces searching for your own and smiling. Here, there was no exclusivity, no one was better than themselves, we were all united, sharing dinner, sharing stories.

Afterwards, I would occasionally join John for a walk, other times I would go to the cinema. I wouldn't stay for the whole film, which was predominantly reruns of 'The Face of The World' but would go for nostalgia.

The air smelled like champagne even though alcohol was not allowed in here and the opening doors seemed black without the presence of Faceless flashes. The carpet was still red but was always desolate and short. The world I once lived in was reduced to something so small.

Chapter Forty Nine

Mark

As the sun grew colder and the days fell short, my team and I were still ploughing on. We had completed half a community with more projects on the way. We were laying down the foundations of the future.

My hands were sore with the success of themselves. I had sharpened my skills and learned how to mould metal. Will was impressed but said there was something missing.

This is when he told me about the meaning of consequences.

He reminded me that although there had been no rules against it, I had still killed people and this would not be accepted in the new world.

"There is no such thing as a deserved death, just murder. To end someone's life was to destroy and that was evil and would be met with punishment decided by the rest of the society."

He told me about the plans he had for punishment. The culprit would be put in a cavea, in the public eye and be forced to stand in shame for the rest of their life as a sacrifice for taking another.

We were building what he was referring to as an Ulicosr. It was a bullish brute of a building. One tall watching eye tower and several small glass rooms with cold metal reinforcements. A danger on display that spectators would be encouraged to stare at as the monster within them repented, always being watched.

A constant spotlight scalding you forever, scanning for shame in your soul and instilling you with it until you buckled and burned. The floor was littered with needles and nails, sharp end up, placed just uncomfortably enough that if you did buckle under the weight of your own choices your fingertips and footbeds would befriend pain until it was all they knew.

I pleaded with Will to not subject me to the pain of my own creation but he said it had to be done. He said he knew I would sometimes still tremble with the pain of my past, still searching for the imprisoned whisky.

He knew of my murders and said he was being merciful by only sentencing me to the room for 2 days.

After 12 hours my eyes began to water, and my calves began to buckle but I told myself that I was stronger than this. I stayed upright, I stayed smiling, blinking out the light in my eyes.

As my skeleton began to scream at me, I imagined Jill, how thankful she would be that I was in here. I was learning, I was trying to redeem myself, not to win her back but to build a better world for her to live in. I would hope, in time, she would forgive me.

I thought of her touch, thought of her laughter, thought of the birds she would sit and count as I rushed off to the projects.

I know she liked the blue ones, they were little and quick and full of song. I thought of that now, humming the tune as she often did. My eyes were not watering now but weeping, wishing that I had sung along with her, wishing she had taught me the names of the birds so I could list them now and think more deeply of her.

I had mistaken Jill's silence for lack of interest and stupidity, but really it had been her vice, her peace, her empathy.

I felt hands on my back and for a fleeting moment the bite of nails in my toes. I screamed as Will dragged me out and took me up to the house.

 He got me a coffee and sat me down, calling the doctor in for a blanket which she wrapped around me before administering some sort of numbing liquid into my mouth.

"Mark, I have pulled you out early as I believe what I am about to tell you may come as a bigger punishment, although it is one I am sorry to deliver."

I nodded and rubbed at my swollen eyes.

"Mark, Jill's body has been found washed up on shore. She dead."

I didn't register the sound his mouth had made for a while but I felt myself slump into a heap like tired clothes at the end of the day, a miserable muddle on the floor.

"Mark, I am very sorry to have to tell you this, I want you to know that your wellbeing is my priority."

He was a distant hum, a radiator in the room down the corridor that needed tending too, burbling. Jill, something sad about Jill.

"Put me back in the cavea."

Will was silent.

"Please put me back in that place and tell me this is not true. I would take an eternity on my feet to let her walk again. I don't want her to be dead, is that enough Will? Can I bring her back? I don't want her to be dead."

"But she wanted it, Mark. I am going to give you rest, I am going to give you your days to weep and then you are to build a burial ground. Her body can be the first you place in it and then you must bury the people you murdered and you will never bury a body again."

In her life Jill had become a ghost to me, shrinking in and out of existence in response to my presence, she only lived for me and I never loved her properly.

She had floated, drifting through her days like a leaf in the tide, not defiant, not demanding difference, just allowing simplicity to wash over her.

I wondered why she had done what she did, but feared I would fall at the explanation. Perhaps I should have gone back again as a changed man or made her another bird box.

Perhaps I should have reached out to the boy and tried to act as a father figure to him. I should have tried harder, I should have made my love for her my focal point instead of a fleeting afterthought.

I knew all that was left to do was apologise and repent. I resorted to redeem myself by living honestly and authentically for her.

I convinced myself that Jill was still living inside of me, her peace filled my bones and soothed me as I sobbed into the sleepless nights, her soul still lingering on. I would keep her beauty alive in the buildings I would create. All standing as a shrine to her.

I laid her to rest along with the other nameless bodies and carved her stone to read 'wife, mother and believer'.

I bought some wood and metal netting and built what became a bird sanctuary around their bodies, rescuing birds, several of them the little blue ones she liked.

Sometimes, between the bricks and the blistering sun, in the early mornings I would sing with the birds, counting each one so she knows her memory will go on.

Chapter Fifty

Florence

Young minds, young faces, imagination that transports you to unseen places. After a year of teaching, Will got me a spot as a director. It was a trial run but I had proved my due diligence to him whilst inspiring generations to step outside of themselves, still holding on to their own hands as they became someone else.

I orchestrated their plays, I wrote their scripts, but more importantly, I listened to their suggestions, explaining why I was agreeing or why I wasn't.

I met up with my friend who had produced my first failure as an actress. She was working as a dressmaker now, producing clothes for the workers and hiring models to walk for her.

Between fittings and sewing needles, she still took the time to write plays but had been working on one for over 6 months and had started fading from the pages.

She chuckled when I encouraged her to pick it up again as I wanted to do right by her. I wanted to give her, her moment. I joked that she could even do costume design for the film, I would just direct it.

I had to persuade Will to fund it, pleading with him that the cinema was a portal to possibility, a fuel that when poured onto production would create progress.

"Leaving the cinema you feel transformed, you feel indomitable, there is power in that seat and you let it possess you."

"I don't want people to feel empowered so that they lose focus, I want them to feel pride and purpose, a sense of joy in their duties."

"Will, need I remind you that one of the major reasons we are talking today is because of a film I was a big producer of, I can do that again."

He found me a camera operator, actors and artists for set designs the next day.

No longer was I restricted in my pursuit, I could explore multiple options. I was free of being driven by one predominant want and greedy with what I deserved. I wanted to tell my own stories and other people's. I wanted to empower the next generation and speak out against corrupt Faceless, encouraging those who remained faithful to rise up against its obfuscation and take back ownership of oneself.

I had been just a mere actress under the Faceless, fed my own desires and driven mad by the demands of them. My insatiable need to portray others driven by a Faceless that had no understanding of my complexities or the toll my own needs would take on me. Without it, I was free to be who I needed to be.

I still stand on stages but I share them with others, I share stories of when I was famous and why I chose to flee from that life.

Chapter Fifty One

John

Teaching taught me that I was talented just not in the way I had once thought. My talent was seeing the smile on the faces of the children I taught, hearing the words I had taught them flow from their mouths as they formed sentences for the first time.

I didn't write anymore, perhaps I never really had done. I had been selfish, I had focused solely on what I wanted instead of what my fellows needed from me. Of course, I had my space days but I spent these volunteering or with Florence, both of us speaking about our excitement for our days of devotion, working again to build a better future.

I wonder if they still use the Faceless in the city? Florence says there are a few rogue agents but I think this may just be another story of hers.

I can't travel to check, the state doesn't change for me now, I often wonder if it was even real. Although it must have been as there is occasionally music in my mind and I think of Jada.

Of course, there are times late at night when the sky is open and the stars are sparkly and I remember the Stellar Chronicles, I remember Synthetic Skies and I dream of who I once was.

Chapter Fifty Two

Will

There are now no Basis, there is only pride in production and in fruition. I saved the children from the streets, reduced self-deaths and invented murder. I saved others from themselves by granting them guidelines and giving them opportunities to find success through connection. You will always find yourself, I just put steps in place to get there.

People once believed they could do what they desired just by wanting it enough but enough is never enough when you can always want more.

Others were told they could have whatever they wanted but were never taught to want anything, convinced they could want the wrong things and still be a good person.

Some were lied to, told they were talented when they weren't, humiliated in the face of those better than them, seeing their talent as a threat rather than a learning opportunity hence why they struggled, they suffered and they sentenced themselves to silence.

My people know their place. They know they are not better than anyone because everyone is the same. My world has granted them the same opportunities and instead of wanting it, they must work for it.

Self-indulgence no longer reigns over their psyche, they are more in tune with their society. I have given them what they wanted, guidance, fulfilment, connections and in return I got what I wanted, change.

396

About the author- C. L. Lomas

Always building up other worlds by imagining what if and asking why, I thought I would share one with you, hence my debut novel What You Wanted. Thank you so much for reading!

Please reach out to me on TikTok @c.l.lomas to follow my creative journey, join a community of creatives, or simply to find a good book to read.

Through passion, perseverance and patience many things can be achieved.